the only World you get

ARKANSAS STORIES

America is an enormous country and it has more than its fair share of extraordinary fiction writers, so it's inevitable that many of them don't receive the readership and acclaim they deserve. Dennis Vannatta is one such writer. He is an absolute master of the colloquial American voice, especially the mid-South variety, and he has an uncanny gift for creating compelling characters who unconsciously reveal their all-too-human flaws. His stories pulse with longing and loss despite the fact that their narrators often attempt to hide their emotions with stoicism, cynicism, and humor. *The Only World You Get* is a superb collection of stories, and luckily, it's not the only Dennis Vannatta book you can get. I urge you to enter not only the world of this book but also the worlds he maps in his four previous story collections and his novel. If you do, I'm sure you'll add him to your list of your favorite contemporary fiction writers.
—David Jauss, *Glossolalia: New & Selected Stories*

Who knows why some books find a place on the shelf of every serious reader, while others, just as powerful and enlightening, do not, but Dennis Vannatta is famous to me. If literary merit and literary success were one and the same, then surely the writer of such quiet masterpieces as *Around Centralia Square* and *Lives of the Artists* would be a household name. I turned to this new collection as eagerly as I have to all his others.
—Kevin Brockmeier, *The Illumination and A Few Seconds of Radiant Filmstrip*

Dennis Vannatta demonstrates once again his remarkable gifts as a writer of short fiction. His unique and finely-tuned voice expresses the comic-seriousness of everyday experience in an amusing, sad, and poignant way. Like all true artists, he sees the unusual in the usual, the lofty in the lowly, and the marvelous in the mundane. Don't miss him.
—Phillip McMath, *The Broken Vase* (winner of the Worthen Prize for fiction)

As intimate as Raymond Carver's stories are, and as wry as Flannery O'Connor's, *The Only World You Get* has its own unique flavor. In this outstanding collection, Dennis Vannatta reveals the very heart of the American heartland—and it turns out to be a far more complex place than people on the coasts tend to think. Always entertaining and often poignant, this collection confirms what we already knew about Vannatta: that he belongs in the company of Charles Portis and Donald Harington, as one of the truest tale-tellers of The Natural State.
—Gary Craig Powell, *Stoning the Devil*

DENNIS VANNATTA lives in Little Rock, Arkansas, where he is retired from three decades in the English Department at The University of Arkansas at Little Rock. He has published stories in many magazines and anthologies, including *Chariton Review, Boulevard, Antioch Review,* and *Pushcart XV.*

the only World you get

ARKANSAS STORIES

DENNIS VANNATTA

et alia press

Little Rock, Arkansas
2016

Copyright © 2016 Et Alia Press
All rights reserved. No part of this book may be reproduced without permission
of the publisher.

Published in the United States of America by:
Et Alia Press
1819 Shadow Lane
Little Rock, AR 72207
Etaliapress.com

ISBN: 978-1-944528-90-4
Library of Congress Control Number: 2016955752

Cover Image by Walter Arnold © 2012
Cover Design by Amy Ashford, Ashford Design Studio, ashford-design-studio.com
Layout Design by Kathy Oliverio
Edited by Erin Wood

This is a work of fiction. Names, characters, places and incidents either are the
product of the author's imagination or are used fictitiously. Any resemblance to
actual persons, living or dead, events, or locales is entirely coincidental.

Acknowledgments:
"Deer Whistle" appeared in slightly different form in *The Minnetonka Review*;
"Fireflies" in *Clackamus Literary Review*; "A Sky-Blue Cadillac" in *Prairie Winds*;
"Afterglow" in *Otoliths*; "Pamplona" in *Edge*; "History 232" in *Descant*; "Traveling
Light" in *Eclipse*; "At the Old Ballgame" in *South 85*; "Rag and Bone" in *Big
Muddy*; and "To the Fordyce Bathhouse" in *William and Mary Review*.

For those rascals, Andrew and William

TABLE OF CONTENTS

DEER WHISTLE

Currently Doyle Tripp is afraid of deer. There are a lot of them here in Arkansas. Around a month ago, I think it was, I read in the paper about a man from Hampton in the southern part of the state who hit a deer with his Silverado, rolled the damn truck and wound up as dead as he'd ever be. My guess is Doyle saw the same article because right after it came out he shows up with a deer whistle on his pickup.

"They can hear that baby from a mile away. It's like a snow plow, only it clears the road of deer," he explained to me.

"I know what it does, Doyle," I said, "but I swear it drives me right up the damn wall every time I hear that damn screeching."

"Aw, Clayton, come on. You only hear it when I'm coming or going."

How do you reason with a man who says something like that? He wasn't being smart-alecky, either. Doyle isn't that type. He's a nice guy, a good neighbor. This was the first thing I'd complained about, in fact, in the three years I'd lived just down from him out here on Left Fork Road. He was as apologetic as can be, but he still hasn't taken that damn deer whistle off his pickup.

Doyle's been by himself too long, that's what I figure. Until I bailed out on Sara and moved into this little mobile home a hundred yards down the blacktop from his house, Doyle hadn't lived within earshot of another human being since his wife got electrocuted out at the shoe factory, oh, how long ago? The shoe factory's been closed for at least a dozen years, so longer than that.

He's odd, no getting around it. Odd but not crazy. It's not crazy to be afraid of dying. Who isn't? But you can take it to the extreme. He'll read about something or hear something or just dream it all up on his own, something that scares him so that it's all he can think about, and he'll stay scared of whatever it is until some new thing comes along. They average about one a season, I'd guess, which means this deer thing has another couple of months to run. I don't know if I can last that long.

Hell, if I'd wanted noisy neighbors, I would've just stayed in Prospect. It may be a little town, but every direction you turn there'll be a person there, so Prospect might as well be New York City, the way I see it. And I'm not living in New York City.

That's where Sara is right now, far as I know. She came to see me before she headed east, the only visitor I've had since I moved out here except for Doyle, who's come over a bunch of times with tomatoes and other stuff from his garden, but he never got all the way inside. Come to think of it, neither did Sara. Not that there's anything wrong with her. Sara's a good woman, no complaints from me, nothing about our split her fault, I'll be the first to say it. It's just that a relationship takes a lot of energy to keep going, and my needle was on empty.

Anyway, one day there she is at my door, says she's come to say goodbye, says she's given up on us, can't invest any more of her life waiting to see if I'll come around (we'd been broke up for around six months by then), so she might as well follow her dream and go to New York City and see if she can make it big in acting.

I'm not making this up. She was forty-three when she lit out, a year older than me, a couple of kids by the time she was eighteen without benefit of marriage, both fathers vamoosed. She raised those girls on her own, working two jobs most of the time, waitress, school cook, highpoint being the manager of the cleaners on Main in Prospect. Both kids turned out to be sluts, but you can't blame Sara for that, and at least they were out of her hair not long after they were old enough to go on birth control. The point is, Sara was no starry-eyed teenager, falling for that "break into acting" crap.

I told her, too. "Hell, goddamn it, Sara, think about it. How many movies and TV shows have you seen where some dumb broad from the sticks heads for Hollywood or New York to make it big and winds up being on the streets, white slavery, something like that?"

"Oh, so you're worried about me now?" she said. I'd been all set to say something nice to her because like I said she's a damn good woman on the whole, I bear no grudges, but I had to watch my step here, she was on the lookout for options, but I wasn't. So I didn't say anything.

She just looked at me for a minute and when that didn't get anything out of me she said, "It's not like I'm doing so great here," and when I didn't say anything to that, either, she added, "and neither are you."

That's when I said, "Fine. There's nothing holding you here. Enjoy your bite of the Big Apple, you silly bitch," and slammed the door, because from my experience it's better to make the break clean.

I haven't heard from her since then. I thought she might call on my birthday or maybe Christmas, but not a word. If she was hard up, she could have called collect. I would have accepted the charges. And if she was too proud for that, a postcard isn't going to break the bank. My guess is she's ashamed because she's not doing too well, not as well as I am for damn sure.

I'm living the goddam American dream, thanks to Lady Luck and the Teamsters Union. I'd held about as many two-bit jobs as Sara before I caught on with UPS. That's how I met Sara, delivering packages to First-Run Video when she was clerking there. They pay you good, UPS, but you earn it, too. Tight schedule, always on the run, climbing into and out of that truck in all weather, wearing those silly-ass shorts. What made it worse was that the UPS office I worked out of was in Marseilles, on up US 65 from Prospect, so I had that half-hour commute onto both ends of all that driving on the job. I'd been at it a year before I met Sara and then another three years after that, and that was three or four years too much for me. I was looking for a way out when the way found me: stepped down out of the truck wrong and wrenched my back somehow. It hurt like hell for a couple of weeks. I could hardly walk, much less work. I was pretty much back to normal in a month, though, but did I tell the company doc that? Ha. My mama didn't raise no fool. The great thing about back pain is that doctors can't tell when you're faking it. Add the support of those fine fellows at the Teamsters Union, and it adds up to permanent disability, check coming in once a month, me never having to work another day in my life.

If it wasn't for that damn deer whistle of Doyle's, life would be grand.

"It's up to orange now, the security thing," I tell him.

"What thing?" Doyle says.

"You know, the security thing. The color thing. The president announces it, colors to tell you how bad things have gotten, you know, green or blue or something for when things are all hunky-dory, then yellow if you have to worry, then orange when it's time to bend over and kiss your ass goodbye. Well, now it's orange."

We're standing on Doyle's front porch. I hadn't even given him a chance to invite me in but just started right in on the orange business that I'd heard about on TV, only I hadn't rehearsed what I was going to say or anything, forget what the hell you call it, and wind up stammering like a damn idiot while Doyle looks at me like I'm speaking Chinese. But then I can tell by the "ah ha" look on his face that he's finally figured it out.

"You mean the security alert, the terrorist business. They've bumped it up to orange, right?"

"You got it. That's it. They were talking about it on TV."

Which is true. You can't just go around making things up with a guy like Doyle, always on the lookout for something to be scared of. He keeps an eye out for stuff like that, reads the papers, listens to the radio, watches the news on TV. You don't want to destroy your credibility by getting caught in a lie.

I go on: "The only reason that I mention it is that they're worried that the A-rabs might be changing their tactics, might start targeting smaller towns now, poison water supplies, stuff like that. I mean, hell, what if they poisoned our goddamn water, Doyle?"

He turns white. No, I'm not just saying that. He really does turn white, and his eyes roll up and he stands there like that with his eyes up like he's studying the underside of the porch roof—bead-board, I notice, a damn expensive cut of wood to use on a porch.

Doyle's house is small, not much bigger if you leave the porch off than my mobile home, but you could tell that back in the day he and his wife kept it fixed pretty nice, vinyl siding, double-hung storm windows, and wall-to-wall carpeting, which I can see through the front door. I've never been inside although he's invited me over for supper and stuff. Like I said, Doyle's a heck of a nice guy, friendly guy, lonely now that his wife's gone and never had any kids, and he'd have me living over here probably if I didn't keep my guard up. Not queer, oh hell no I'm not saying that, but needy, and you can get in over your head real fast with some needy SOB, which is why I kept turning down invites to supper, until he got the point and quit making them.

Finally Doyle gets himself under control and says, "Yeah, I think I did hear something about that. Jesus, Clayton. Our water. What on earth would we do if they got into our water?"

"Die, that's what."

He swallows hard like he's trying to keep something down. "Clayton," he says. "A man's body is eighty percent water, did you know that?"

"Ninety percent's what I heard," I say.

I feel bad about scaring the poor guy, but he's the one who started it. A guy's got a right to a little peace and quiet, doesn't he? Besides, Doyle's going to be scared of something, so why not try to make it something a little easier on the ears?

You have to be careful it doesn't boomerang on you and you wind up with something worse than a deer whistle, of course, but I can't see that happening with water. Hell, I figure enough Tennessee sour mash will kill whatever those A-rabs stick in the water. Not that I'm a juicer or anything. Sure, I'll have a few, but if I drink too much I'll get stupid, start missing Sara. It happened once and I found myself telephone in hand trying to call her in New York, only I didn't know the number. She still has family around Prospect who'd know, but by the time I'd thought of that, the mood had passed. Just as well. If you're not on that ship when it sails, you're not going to catch it swimming.

Thinking about my old pal Jack Daniels makes me thirsty, and I have one or three while I'm watching Doyle's house for signs that my little plot is working.

It's after noon before he comes out, gets in his pickup, and heads off in the direction of town. He's back an hour or so later, and he proceeds to unload must be two dozen plastic gallons of what even from this distance I can tell is distilled water. I figure that bastard will be buying distilled water the rest of his life, probably take baths in it. And that deer whistle is still on his pickup screeching away. So there's one idea shot to hell.

I'm over at Doyle's house again by seven the next morning. I'm not usually an early bird, but I'd had a lousy night trying to sleep so I thought I might as well get up and put Plan B in motion.

The problem last night was this dream. Probably too much Mr. Daniels. I thought I'd learned my lesson. It wasn't Sara this time, though, I wasn't dreaming about her. It was about two kids. There were two kids in the house. Yeah, in this dream I was living in a house right here where the mobile home sits, little house, about the size of Doyle's. I'm going through the house calling,

"Come out, kiddies, kiddies, come out!" Like hide 'n seek or something. Then it's the second part of the dream and the kids are going through the house calling, "Come out, Clayton, Clayton, come out!" A boy and a girl, I think, but I don't see them too clearly now that the dream is over. Not my kids, either. If they were my kids, they'd be calling me "Daddy," not "Clayton," you can bet your ass on that. Not that I've had kids or ever will. Could you see me with kids? Pardon me while I laugh.

Anyway, the dream bugged me for some reason and I couldn't sleep, so here I am on Doyle's porch. For all I know he's still in bed. No, he comes to the door after about two knocks, fully dressed, and before he can say howdy-do I hit him with, "This is the week for orange, looks like."

"Orange? You mean—"

"No no, that was yesterday, that orange alert thing. This is something new. I saw it on CNN, I think it was, or maybe not CNN but one of those stations. Agent orange this time."

"Oh sure, I know all about that, Clayton. I—"

"No you don't. This is something new. They're now finding out that this stuff can take thirty years before it shows up. Guys who thought they were off the hook are now coming down with it bad, real bad."

Doyle doesn't turn white like he did yesterday. Instead he looks off into the distance sort of sad-like. "Oh," he says, "that's awful. That's just awful."

"Yes sir, it is. Soon as I heard it I said to myself, you've got to tell Doyle this. I remember you telling me you were in the army back then and all."

"Well," Doyle says, looking down like he's sort of embarrassed or something.

"You should get it checked out, Doyle. It may not be too late. There might be something they can do for you yet."

"Well," he begins again, "you know, Clayton, I spent my whole tour of duty stateside. I was one of the lucky ones."

"Oh yeah," I say, off kilter for a second, but I'm fast on my feet and come right back with, "But that's the bad thing about all this, Doyle. They now think this stuff is potent enough that even if you weren't exposed to it yourself but were just around some poor bastard who was, you know, like sleeping next to him in the barracks or something, you could come down with it, too. Those are the guys who're getting hit with it now after all these years, the ones who were exposed to it second-hand. Now I may have this all wrong, but that's how I understood it, anyway. CNN, I think it was."

I add the bit about maybe being wrong because I'm strictly winging it at this point, of course. But Doyle doesn't hardly seem to be paying attention to me anyway. He's staring off into the distance again with that sad look, so sad I turn for a look, too, but there's nothing there.

When I turn back, Doyle is looking at me now, and he says, "Clayton, you know I lost a brother over there, over in Nam."

And I say, "Doyle, we all lost brothers over there."

"No," he says, "I lost my *brother*, Clayton, my brother Leslie. My baby brother—"

Then he can't talk. He's not crying exactly, but he has tears in his eyes and he can't talk.

"I'm sorry, Doyle," I say, and I am, too. I never meant for it to go like this. All I wanted was for him to take that damn deer whistle off his pickup.

I feel so bad that I'm just about to reach out and give him a pat on the arm, comforting, you know? But a guy in an emotional state like Doyle can go from being sad to jumping up and busting you in the chops in about half a second. So I keep my hands to myself, turn around and head for home, trying not to break into a run.

Half an hour later he's knocking on my door, says he's heading down to the veterans' cemetery in Little Rock to put flowers on Leslie's grave, wants to know if I want to come along. Little Rock's ninety minutes each way. They can keep Little Rock far as I'm concerned, keep it and welcome to it. I'm not wasting three hours on the road to see that mess. I make some excuse that sounds lame even to me, but hell, why should I feel guilty? He's not my damn brother, is he?

I don't believe in any third time's the charm bullshit, but the next day I give it one final try anyway. Why? Couldn't tell you. Maybe just boredom. Maybe meanness. I wouldn't put much of anything past me.

It was a little bit of trivia I read in the "Food" section of the paper this morning while I was eating my oatmeal. About tomatoes. I'd heard it before, but when I saw it this time naturally I thought of Doyle because he raises them. Good ones. He'll bring me over a sack full a couple of times a week during the bearing season. More than I can eat. Enough for a whole family.

"I've got to stop watching CNN," I tell him when he comes to the door. He doesn't say a word but just looks at me, waiting. I can tell what he's thinking, though. He's thinking he's damn sorry he rented the mobile home to my sorry ass.

Maybe I forgot to mention that Doyle's my landlord. He bought the mobile home, used, and parked it out here for his mother to live in after his father died. Then his mother died of breast cancer. Then a year later his wife gets electrocuted out at the shoe factory. Or maybe it was the other way around, wife first, then mother. Whatever. He rents the mobile home to me. Said he'd be glad of the company. I'll bet he'd sing a different tune now.

Anyway, he stands there looking at me like, Please God, somebody put me out of my misery, and I tell him, "It's tomatoes they were talking about last night. I mean to tell you I have got to stop watching that damn CNN. *Tomatoes*. Innocent thing like that. Who would think they'd be the thing to do you in?"

I give him an opening, but nothing from Doyle, so I go on. "Guess what? Tomatoes are a member of the Deadly Nightshade family. Deadly Nightshade! Poison! Yeah yeah yeah, I know they've known that for years, but now they're beginning to think that folks back in the olden days who thought tomatoes were poison, too, were on to something. A tomato now and then won't bother you at all, but you eat too much of them and over the years the poison can build up and, well, they're not sure what it'll lead to down the road, but whatever it is, it's not good, you can bet on that."

That's it, I'm done, game over. I just stand there waiting for whatever he's going to say or do, call me a goddamn liar, kick my ass off his property, whatever, it's all the same to me.

But he just looks at me a moment, then looks down at the ground or whatever and smiles. There are smiles that are real smiles, happy smiles, and then there are smiles that are about the saddest damn things in the world. This was one of the sad ones.

Then he says, "It was Nancy planted that garden—the first time, I mean. Planted tomatoes, lettuce, radishes, carrots, green peppers, cucumber—different things over the years. But she started with tomatoes first off. Said you couldn't beat a good tomato. Hell, it didn't make any difference to me, not at first. Store-bought was fine with me. But she was right. A fresh tomato is something. Early Girl. Better Boy. That's what Nancy planted. She just liked the names. She called them her boys and girls. I'll still plant a couple of Better Boys and Early Girls for old time's sake, but I'll grow Beefsteak, too, and try out one of the newer hybrids every year. You can't beat Better Boy and Beefsteak for taste, but those new hybrids are good in Arkansas, what with all the bugs and wilt and stuff we get here."

I wait for him to go on because, like I said, I'm shot, I'm through, but for the longest time he doesn't say anything else, just stands there looking down with that sad, sad smile. Then finally when things are starting to get a little uncomfortable he looks up at me and says, "You know, Clayton, everybody I ever loved died. Every single one."

He isn't crying, either. No tears in his eyes. Not yet, anyway.

❋

I pull the back off the La-Z-Boy so it's easier to carry and haul it in two trips into the bedroom end of the mobile home that's got the window looking out on Doyle's house. I sit in comfort all day long, watching.

Doyle finally comes out at sunset right when, you know how it gets sometimes, when the sun's sitting on the edge of the world, the light slanting straight across everything, everything either in shadow like it was cut out of black construction paper or lit up so bright you think you can see right through it. Doyle's lit up, a hundred yards away and I can see him lit up like there's a spotlight on him, see him crying, I swear I can see those tears, as he rips those tomato plants out of the ground one after another and flings them over his shoulder without looking. Well, I knew he'd be crying sometime.

After he finishes with the tomato plants he goes on to the cucumber vines and eggplant or green pepper, I can't tell from here, and then he's down on his hands and knees tearing at something, maybe radishes or carrots, although you'd think it'd be too late in the season for those.

Not that I ever grew anything myself. Sara used to say she wished she'd lived in one place long enough to grow a garden. It was a dream of hers. She'd come in and announce right out of the blue, "Well, today I'd be putting the okra in," or, "It's really wet this summer. I'd be spraying my tomatoes for blossom-end rot right about now." So over the years with Sara I picked up a few things about gardens.

Doyle's halfway down a row of something green when he gets tired of ripping stuff up, I guess, and stands up and brushes his pants off and goes back into the house. I watch awhile more, but I really don't expect to see him out there again. What else is there for him to do? I've messed him up good.

Night falls and I don't feel good about much of anything. I go into the bathroom and break the mirror and then start looking around for more mirrors to break but then say to myself, what the hell, what the hell.

I get a powerful urge to talk to Sara. I get as far as holding the phone in my hand, trying to think who I should call to get her number, when I realize what a dumb idea it is. Sara's got a new guy now. Nobody's ever told me that, but it's a fact anyway. She's the type of person who has to have somebody in her life all the time. So she'll have a new guy.

What the hell.

It gets darker and darker inside the mobile home. You'd think once night falls, that would be it, but somehow it just keeps getting darker. But I don't even put a light on. There's nothing here I want to see.

I sit for a long time in the dark until I can't do that anymore, and then I head over to Doyle's. I don't bother to look at my watch, but I know it's got to be the middle of the night by now, yet his house is lit up, like he's got every light going.

I go up on the porch and knock on the door, and here comes Doyle. He just stares at me, which is a damn sight better than what he should be doing to me. *I'm sorry* is what I came over to say. I'm not sure what I would have said after that. I don't know if I would have had the guts to tell him all I've done, but I would have said *I'm sorry*, at least that.

But before I can work up to getting even that out, Doyle says, "Are you scared, too?"

I nod, and he steps back and I go on in. We're in the living room.

"Here," he says, motioning toward the sofa, and I sit down.

He disappears into another room, then is back in a minute with a pillow, sheet, and a blanket.

"It folds out into a bed," he says, meaning the sofa, "but we'd have to move the furniture around for that. We can do that tomorrow night. Late as it is, this will do you for tonight, won't it?"

I nod, taking the bedding from him. Doyle disappears again, and I start to make up the sofa. When I finish, he still hasn't come back, so I sit there awhile, waiting, until I decide he's gone to bed. I take my shoes off and lie down. I close my eyes for a second, and when I open them, there's Doyle again. He's got this look on his face like, I don't know, like I'm somebody he hasn't seen for a long time.

"It's good to not always be alone," he says. I nod.

He stares at me another minute, and then his expression changes, gets tense or something, like he's just thought of something.

"Tomorrow we'll go into town and buy you a good deer whistle," he says. "OK?"

I nod.

FIREFLIES

I'd just gotten out of the car and was walking across the farmyard toward John Epps's front door when I heard a *bang*, like someone hitting a garbage can with a sledge hammer, and at the same time a moan of pain or rage or despair, or all of them at once. An animal. Except for four years at the state college in Conway and two years in the Army, I've lived all my life in Prospect, Arkansas, population 1,006. You can't walk a hundred feet in any direction from Prospect without stepping on somebody's farm, but that doesn't make me a farmer. Animals? If an animal is bigger than a kitty cat, I don't want any part of it, and I would have beat a fast retreat back to the car and let John Epps come see me in my office if he had business with me, but then I thought *she* might be watching, so I steeled myself and went on up to the front door.

I hadn't gotten all the way through knocking when the door opened and there she was, Trish, my Trish. No, not mine. John's. Trish Epps.

I started to hold out my hand but stopped because I'd read in *Miss Manners* that the man waits for the lady to extend her hand to indicate she wants to shake. Besides, if I extended my hand and Trish wouldn't take it, then what would I do with my hand hanging in the air?

"Hi, Trish."

"He's around there," she said with a kind of circular motion of her head meant to indicate, I guess, around behind the house. She didn't extend her hand. No "Hi, Rick" or "Ricky." She'd called me that once. Trish Springer had called me Ricky once.

"OK," I said, like Lee said OK to Grant at Appomattox.

She couldn't have hurt me any worse if she'd cut my hand off. Not even to call me Ricky when all I'd done is love her this half century, love her every day through wars and presidential assassinations and a wife of my own and kids and grandkids, and I loved them all in my own way, tried my best even if I failed them, but Trish, Trish, not to even call me Ricky. It hurt so.

"OK," I said and raised my hand as if doffing my hat to her, only I wasn't wearing one.

I walked around the house and, *bang!*, came that hammer-on-tin sound again—from a little trailer parked off to the side of the farm lot. I veered off in the other direction. Then here comes John Epps out of a Butler building, big sliding doors on front, probably his tractor shed.

I figured Miss Manners would be OK with me sticking my hand out, so I did, but John didn't take it, so I figured the Lord had set aside this day as one I wasn't going to get my hand shook on. I'd about sworn off shaking anyway after getting two different kinds of the flu last winter, but it seemed a hard thing that John Epps wouldn't shake my hand because when we were pups and ranked our friends one two three he'd always been one or two for me and I'm pretty sure I was the same for him. But that was a long time ago, 1968, our senior year at dear old Prospect High. Go Wildcats. But then things went wrong between us, I'm not exactly sure what, I'm truly not.

It went wrong between him and just about everybody, seems like. I went off to college and never heard a thing more about him except that he and Trish Springer got married about a year later, but I never saw either one of them around town when I came home summer or on breaks, and nobody else I talked to did, either. After college I got lucky number seven in the draft lottery and spent two years in Uncle Sam's legions, then came back and took over for old Auburn Larkin as the Heartland Insurance agent for the Prospect area. I still never heard anything about John or Trish and just kind of assumed they'd moved. But then one day here comes a check from John renewing his farm insurance policy, which I hadn't even realized he had.

Not long after that I ran into Terry Pfeiffer, also a farmer, and he said, sure, he saw John every once in a while at the grain elevator or the farmers' co-op. He'd given up trying to talk to him, though.

"He's a stand-offish bastard. Won't hardly look you in the eye. He's a sharp one when it comes to the dollar, though, I'll grant him that. He's hell for the dollar."

"That just doesn't sound like John."

"No, it don't. He was as nice a guy as you'd ever want to meet in high school."

"How about Trish? You ever see her?"

"Trish?"

"His wife."

"Oh yeah, that's right. He did marry Trish Springer, didn't he? No, I haven't seen Trish Springer in years."

That would have been probably 1974. Where do the years go? They go on wings, I'll tell you that.

I'm not saying I've never seen him or Trish. You can't live in a little community like this without running into people, even if they are trying to be some kind of hermit. Since high school, I've seen my former best friend somewhere around a dozen times. I've seen Trish seven times. I can give you the dates, the places, the time of day. The weather. What she wore. Where she looked when she looked anywhere except at me.

❧

I followed John across the farm lot. He was limping bad. I figured it was just a touch of arthritis since we both were at that age, but then I decided he didn't have the arthritis look on his face, like it's been hurting you so long you've almost forgotten about it. Whatever was hurting John was fresh enough he was still resenting it like hell.

"What happened to you?"

"What do you mean?"

I nodded at his leg. "You're limping."

"Oh. That bitch got a horn into me."

I thought he was talking about Trish and made a fist, although taking a swing at him would have been way down on the list of good ideas. He was always bigger than me, plus he'd spent a lifetime working on a farm while I'd mostly sat behind a desk. If I'd taken a swing at John Epps to defend the good name of my fair lady, I would've ended up looking at that farm lot from a whole different angle.

Fortunately, before I could do something silly, it occurred to me that Trish didn't have a horn. At that moment John stopped and faced the trailer we'd just come along side of—what I'd call a horse trailer although I don't know if that's the name of it—and pointed like a prosecuting attorney and said, "She's in there." She must have heard us talking about her and didn't like it. *Bang*! I took a step back

"What is she?"

"A goddamn non-polled Hereford bitch. I was trying to load her into the chute and she got ornery and got a horn into me. Got me in the groin. Lucky she didn't take my pecker off."

"Must have hurt."

"You think?"

"Did you see a doctor?"

"Damn right. He cleaned it out and stitched me up and gave me a bunch of antibiotics so's it wouldn't get infected. Wanted to put me in the hospital, but a farmer can't go into the hospital any time you get a few stitches sewn into you."

"Still. You gotta be careful with something like that. I had hernia surgery a few years back and the doctor told me I couldn't lift more than ten pounds until it healed, so for a solid month I couldn't take a leak without somebody holding my John Thomas for me."

An old joke. John must have heard it too many times because he didn't laugh.

"So what are you going to do with her?" I said, and he said, "Sell her ass."

"At Grau's? The auction's not until tomorrow, is it? You going to leave her in there until then?"

"Why not? She's already been in there three days. Bitch should be used to it by now."

I started to say something but didn't. I didn't want to sound like some animal rights hothead. That doesn't go over well among farmers. And maybe it doesn't hurt a cow to stay cooped up like that. What do I know?

He turned and hobbled off, and I followed him to an outbuilding closest to the road where we stopped and John nodded down at an open space partly graveled but mostly dirt.

"That's where it was before they took off with it."

"Where what was?" I said before I remembered, oh yeah, why he'd called me out there.

"The disk," he said, not adding "dumb ass" although I could tell it was on the tip of his tongue.

"I thought you told me over the phone it was a harrow."

"Rick, a disk *is* a harrow."

Normally a thing like that would embarrass the hell out of me, but his calling me "Rick" had thrown me off because even John would use my name but Trish wouldn't call me anything. After all she'd been to me.

"So what happened, exactly," I said.

"Well, Rick, if I knew what happened *exactly*, I'd go and get my disk back from whoever stole it. Didn't you get the report I made with Dale Carson?"

Dale is the county sheriff.

"Yeah, it's in the car. Why don't you tell me, though?"

"Well, there's not a hell of a lot to tell. I had it out here because I was working on it, getting it ready to start disking up that bottom land," he said, jerking his thumb over his shoulder. "It was still there this morning when Trish and I ran into Marseilles to the assessor's office. She had a little shopping to do, too. We were gone a couple of hours, back by ten. The disk was gone when we got back."

I eyed the blacktop road. "So they hooked her up behind a tractor and just drove off down the road with her?"

John spat. "Shit. Don't be stupid. They put it on a flatbed."

I felt myself blushing. In some circles around here, being stupid about farm stuff calls your manhood into question.

"I've been working a lot of years, and I've never seen a disk stolen before."

"Well, congratulations. You just busted your cherry."

I don't know why he hates me so. I just don't understand it.

After I'd gotten the call from John about the theft around noontime, I'd gone online and looked up some stuff about harrows—yeah, now I remember, they are called disks—so I wouldn't appear as ignorant as I really am. "Just by coincidence I was at the co-op a week or so ago," I lied, "and old Olin Breckenridge, I believe it was—no, maybe not Olin, somebody, though—said he had a disk for sale. Said he wanted five thousand for it."

John cocked his head. "You telling me you think my disk is worth five thousand dollars?"

Uh oh. Had I stepped in it? Maybe he'd been about to tell me his was worth three thousand.

"I don't know anything about yours, John."

"It's all in the sheriff's report."

"The one that's in my car, you mean? Yeah, I'll get around to reading that sometime."

"You always were a wiseass son of a bitch," he said.

But I wasn't. I've always gotten along with people. And John Epps had been my number one or two best friend. What the hell?

"What kind of disk was Orin, or whoever it was, selling?" John said.

"John Deere. I don't remember what specific model."

John snorted. "That explains it. I wouldn't have a John Deere on my property."

"Yours was a . . .?"

"International Harvester, of course. And it was worth a hell of a lot more than five thousand dollars. It was worth fifteen if a nickel. It's all in the report."

"Guess I'd better go read that report."

"Guess you had."

These farmers get serious about their equipment. Back in high school I'd seen fights between John Deere kids and I.H. kids. A city person would think it was a strange thing, I guess, but everybody's got something. It just all comes down to where the heart leads you, like the heart led John and Trish to becoming virtual hermits out on a farm only three miles from where we all went to high school together. And like it led me back out there after sundown that same night, flashlight in one hand (although I was afraid to put it on) and one-iron in the other in case I came across some animal I couldn't outrun.

It hadn't occurred to me to go back out to John Epps's farm until supper, which I had at my mother's house. My wife waited until the kids were grown and then she moved out on me. No surprise to anybody. We all knew it was coming. We're still friends, which is pretty much all we ever were. A man only has one true love in his life, and I'm sorry for it, Debbie, but you weren't mine.

Anyway, I was having supper with Ma, telling her about my day, and all of a sudden I heard myself saying, "That disk's still out there on John Epps's farm."

"You think so?"

"I know so," I said although until right then I hadn't thought any such thing. Maybe it had been something that had been sort of stewing in the back of my mind, recalling Terry Pfeiffer saying that John was hell for the dollar, then me being a farm insurance agent for the best part of forty years and never hearing of a disk being stolen. Now I know folks'll steal anything not nailed down, but a disk is a cumbersome thing, hard to move, used worth a few thousand dollars and not half that stolen, I'd bet. Not hardly worth the aggravation. Get an insurance settlement, though, and still have the disk to use—hidden somewhere on the farm—not a bad deal, that.

"What are you going to do?" Ma asked, and I said, "Go back out there and look for it." Nobody could have been more surprised to hear it than me.

I parked the car in a turn-out on the blacktop a quarter of a mile from John's farmhouse. I sat there awhile marveling at what a stupid thing I was doing. I'd dealt with plenty of claims over the years I was pretty damn sure were bogus, but I'd never once taken flashlight and one-iron in hand to prove my point. But then I'd never before had a claim filed by the man who married the woman I loved.

I'd known Trish Springer all my life, but I'd never thought anything about her because she was the Baptist preacher's daughter, and I thought preachers were a different breed of human being, and so their daughters must be, too. She was a year younger than me, which means a lot when you're a kid, and she was a mousy little thing, even shier than I was, so I just never thought a thing about her. Then one summer night there was an ice-cream social out on the Baptist Church parking lot, and my family went even though we were Methodists. There were colored lights like Christmas lights strung up on poles around the parking lot, and fireflies winking off in the darkness, and soft summer air that when you're that age and think the whole world is there just for you tastes almost as sweet as homemade ice cream. I took my paper plate of ice cream and cake and looked for a place to sit, and there all by herself on the steps leading up to the side door of the church sat Trish Springer, not looking mousy now but so cute I couldn't hardly breathe. I've never been a brave person. The one brave act I ever did was somehow finding the courage to go sit next to Trish. I don't recall we said much to each other, but there were stars and colored lights like Christmas lights and winking fireflies glinting in her eyes. We ate our ice cream and cake and then dumped our paper plates in the big trash barrel, and then we walked over toward the trees between the parking lot and the cemetery, the trees where the fireflies were. I took her hand and we walked among the trees and the fireflies. I kissed her on the cheek. I think I must have been ten or eleven. Trish a year younger. We hadn't hit puberty yet. This wasn't sex, this was love.

That's basically the whole romance between Trish and me. When we were in high school, I asked her to go to the homecoming basketball game with me— just the game because I knew the Reverend would never let her go to the dance afterward—but she said her daddy wouldn't let her date yet, so I thought, OK, I'll wait until she's eighteen or out of high school, whichever, because I could wait for Trish.

Then came the end of our senior year and John and I, best friends, hiked up to Lookout Rock on Flint Hill one day just for something to do. We laid out on the rock in the sun talking about this and that—the future, I guess—and then John said, shy-like because all of us guys, us friends, were shy when it came to the subject of girls, hardly any of us were dating, John said that he'd asked Trish Springer to go with him to the spring prom.

"*Trish Springer*," I said, I guess in a way that sounded to John like I thought she was a real dog or something because John said, "Hey, Trish isn't bad. She's a cute girl," and I said, "Of course she is."

Of course she is.

A year later they were married but living like two hermits out on a farm I was, over forty years later, just about to trespass on, flashlight I was too scared to switch on in one hand and in the other a one-iron you'd hold up in a lightning storm because even God couldn't hit it. Even now, looking back on that night, that firefly-lit summer evening, the day on Lookout Rock, I don't understand any of it.

I don't know if he was already out there waiting on me, expecting me, or if he heard my car coming up the road and came out to investigate, but as I came up between two sheds, John stepped out of the night shadows and said, "Rick, what are you doing here."

I'm proud to say I did manage to control my bowels, but it was a close thing.

"Oh, just looking for my golf ball," I said, holding up the one-iron.

"You think I lied to you about the disk, don't you?" he said, and I said, "Well, John, I have to be honest with you, the thought did cross my mind."

We stared at each other awhile, and then I looked away because those stare-down competitions you have as kids I never was any good at and hadn't improved with age. When I looked back he was still staring at me, not angry so much but a look of hurt in his eyes. Then when he finally broke the silence he really threw me for a loop because he said the very thing I'd been thinking, what I should have said: "Rick, what have you got against me? What did I ever do to you?"

"I don't have anything against you, John," I said. And I don't. Never did. Sure, I'm human, and it hurt like hell when he took Trish to the prom, then married her. But I never felt any sense of betrayal because I never told him about how I felt about her. Never told anybody. That was a secret between me and Trish. Now I'm not so sure Trish was in on it.

"Then why was I cut out?" John said. "Why was I in, then at the last minute I was out, out by myself, on my own?"

I just shook my head. What was he talking about? That's exactly what I asked him: "John, what in the hell are you talking about?"

"You know. Don't pretend. I was a Musketeer just like everybody else. Then you all were gone and I was on my own, out of it. You know damn good and well what I'm talking about. Kid Day."

"Kid—?"

Then it came to me, came to me a little bit at a time because it was so long ago. May, 1968, the last day of classes before high school graduation. Some folks called it Kid Day and some Senior Skip Day because although technically we were supposed to be in class, it was a tradition that the seniors would skip school and dress up some half-ass way, like cowboys or in diapers, some guys in dresses, ride around town throwing water balloons and lighting firecrackers, stuff like that. There were five of us buddies, the Five Musketeers we called ourselves. Clever, hey?

I don't really remember much of what we did Kid Day, but I do recall we met after school the afternoon before, and Larry Utley said we should spend the night out in his granddad's barn, sleep on the hay, have a big ol' time. Only John wasn't there at that moment—late getting out of class or something—and when somebody asked where he was, I said, "Aw, he's off with his lady love someplace. He's got better things to do." I swear I didn't say it to be mean or cut him out but because I really meant it. I would rather have been with Trish Springer than with that bunch of sad sacks, I'll tell you that. Anyway, we took off without him, ate burgers at Y'All Come Inn for supper, then headed out to Virgil Utley's barn. Harold Miner brought a six-pack of Hamm's. It was the first beer I'd ever drunk. Tried to drink. I got through half of one. Harold finished mine, in fact drank most of that six-pack because none of the rest of us were drinkers and Harold apparently wasn't much of one either because before the night was over he vomited up his beer and hamburger, too. When I think of Kid Day, 1968, I think of the smell of beer-vomit on fresh hay.

John hadn't missed much, it seemed to me, but apparently that wasn't what he thought from the look on his face.

Surely, come on, surely that wasn't what did it—turned an aw-shucks nice guy like John Epps into a virtual hermit, poisoned him on everything in the world except Trish, and then he'd poisoned her against the world, too. Or at least against me. And all because he'd missed out on Kid Day? No no no. Explanations for a life can't be that simple. Can't be that stupid. Or maybe there just can't be explanations at all, not where the heart comes in. The heart catches fire, and it burns, and the less sense it makes the hotter it burns.

We just stared at each other. There was the full moon in his eyes, making him look like a crazy man. That same moon was in mine, too, I guess.

I was in my office the next morning with John Epps's papers on the desk in front of me about ready to sign off on the thing when the phone rang. She didn't call me Ricky this time, either.

"You're not going to stop until you find that disk, are you." She said it like a statement, not a question, like I was Sherlock Holmes or something and once I got hold of a case I'd shake it like a dog shaking a blacksnake until it was dead at its feet. In fact, just about the last thing on my mind had been going out to look for that disk again, but because it was Trish on the phone, everything changed.

"I suspect not," I said.

I could hear her sigh. "OK, then. You might as well come on out and get this over with. Come on out right now. Before John gets back."

I said OK. I was surprised I could make it sound as calm as I did.

I drove out there and parked off to the side of the blacktop where I had the night before—in case John returned early, I suppose; I don't know what I was thinking—and walked up the road to the farmhouse. Trish was standing outside the front door waiting for me.

"I guess you aren't going to give up until you find it, are you," she said again, like she needed confirmation before proceeding.

"I guess not."

"It's just that he needs the money. You know what beef prices have been doing. Hogs, too."

"It's the anti-red-meat crowd," I said. She nodded.

We walked across the farm lot, then she opened a gate to the pasture and followed me through and closed the gate, and we walked on across the pasture. We didn't say a word to each other. Sometimes I'd let her get a step ahead of me so I could look at her out of the corner of my eye. Closing in on sixty now. Looks it. So what? Oh love, love, love.

We had to climb through the fence on the east side of the pasture, Trish holding the wire up for me because I guess she figured I didn't even know how to do that on a farm. Then the ground rose a bit and then fell toward a copse of trees with a big cottonwood on one end, and beyond the cottonwood there was a deep cut into the earth, erosion or a natural gully, I don't know, but the end of the gully closest to the cottonwood was filled with brush.

"It's down under that," Trish said as we stood on the edge of the gully looking down. "The disk."

"I can't see it."

"John pushed a lot of brush off onto it. He used a blade on the I.H."

"Yeah, it would have taken something like that," I said like I knew what I was talking about. I squinted down into the brush another minute and then said, "Well, I'm going to have to get down into that and see if I can identify the disk. But it's only so the company won't be liable for the loss. That's my job. I won't turn John over to the law, though, Trish."

She didn't say anything.

I climbed down and started pulling limbs and branches away. I'd thought it was a pleasant morning, but it was hot work under the sun. It'd been an unusually dry spring, and soon the air was filled with dust from me slinging that dead brush around, and I was sneezing and sweating. I don't know how long I was at it. I'd dug down deep enough that that the level of the brush around me was above my head in places. I could finally catch a glimpse of something metallic gleaming down under the brush but couldn't tell for sure what it was. I was hot, beat.

I was all ready to say, There she is, the disk, I see it, although I hadn't for sure seen it when I heard a sound like something splashing above me, and then there was a *whoosh* and a bright light, and even though I was looking at it all around me I swear until I smelled it I didn't realize it was fire.

I started clawing at the brush, trying to fight my way out of there, throwing branches left and right, coughing, cussing, screaming, took me ten minutes it seemed like although it couldn't possibly have been more than a few seconds or that fire would have got me for sure.

Then somehow I was to the bank of the gully, half-running half-crawling up the crumbly side, blinded by the smoke, coughing, choking, then up out of the gully with the fire safely behind me but still terrified because I knew John had to be out there waiting to go upside my head with a spade or gut me with a corn knife of just blow me to kingdom come with a double-barrel, I wouldn't put anything past somebody who'd toss kerosene at a man and try to set him on fire.

I just ran, ran as fast as a totally-exhausted coughing wheezing half-blinded sixty-year-old could run. I ran across the pasture. My vision cleared enough that I saw cows on the west side of the pasture next to the road, where I was headed. I was too scared of John to be afraid of them. "Out of my way, you sons of bitches!" I hollered, and those cows moved fast, like I was the scariest sight they'd seen in many a day.

I climbed through the fence, didn't need anybody to hold the wire for me. Got in my car and started it up and did a U-turn and barreled down the road away from John Epps's farm. I was a menace behind the wheel, eyes still smarting and teary from the smoke, but I could see well enough that, a mile or so on down the road, I saw John in his pickup, that horse trailer behind it, pass me going the other way. Coming back from the auction. Then I finally figured out who set the fire. Anybody else would have known it from the get-go. Anybody not blinded by smoke and dust and fireflies.

Most folks around here call them lightning bugs. I call them fireflies because that summer night—it must have been 1959, 1960, around then—when I took Trish's hand but didn't know what to do next, she said to me, "Let's go walk among the fireflies, Ricky." I think it was the way she said "among the fireflies"— that's when I fell in love with her.

My earliest memories of fireflies were when I was a very little boy out in the back yard with my older sister, Fayrene, chasing lightning bugs, she called them. Fayrene caught one and pinched off its light and came at me with it, saying, "It's gonna burn you, gonna burn!"

I just stood there because I couldn't believe my older sister, whom I adored, would hurt me. But then she grabbed my wrist and I started to send up a howl before she stuck the light on my finger and said, "There, you got you a wedding ring." Oh, how beautiful. But then it began to fade, and I ran after Fayrene, pleading, "Burn me, Sis, burn me."

Like they say, be careful what you wish for.

A Sky-Blue Cadillac

At 10:51 in the morning (I looked at my watch so that I'd always remember the time), our mother stopped breathing. Those of us around her bedside in the hospital—me, my sister Janice (everyone called her Ruby because of her red hair), our little brother Bobby, and our cousin Harlan Lee—stopped breathing, too. Then Bobby opened his mouth to let out that wail we all knew would come to herald our mother's death because even at fifty-five he'd never been able to stop himself—crybaby, crybaby—but it wasn't Bobby who broke the silence. It was our mother. She opened one eye and said in a voice that was stronger, clearer than it had been in days, "Had you going there for a minute, didn't I?"

How we laughed, and even Mother drew her lips out in something like a smile, all she had strength for because this was, after all, the death watch.

"That's Lou for you, ain't it? Ain't that Lou?" Harlan said, reaching over with his open palm as if he were going to slap her on the shoulder but thinking better of it and pulling his hand back. He'd always called her Lou even though she was as much a mother to him as to any of us. The rest of us called her Mother. She insisted on it. Once Bobby, who called his wife "Mom" in front of their kids, without thinking about it called Mother "Mom," and she whirled on him and snarled, "I'm your *mother*, not your *mom*!" Maybe it has something to do with being a woman from the Ozark hill country, with precious few opportunities to assert your dignity.

A year older than Bobby and two years younger than Ruby, which would make him four years younger than me, Harlan came to live with us when he was three. I never was sure exactly why. In our family we make it a habit of not talking about what needs to be talked about. It had something to do with Harlan's mother, no doubt, a wild one, married I don't know how many times. I think she must have already been split up from Harlan's dad. I don't remember much about him, just that he was one of that ornery Lee bunch. Mother and Aunt Belle never got along. When Aunt Belle finally showed up to reclaim her son years later, Harlan cried and held onto Mother's leg until Mother, crying herself, pulled his hands loose, and then he scrambled over to the kitchen table and held on to that leg, too, and they couldn't pry him off it. Finally my dad—a giant of a man, strong as an ox until drink and smoking did him in—picked up the whole table and held it in the air until Harlan lost his hold, and then Aunt Belle pounced on him.

Harlan came back to us a number of times after that, the "visits" lasting from a few weeks to over a year. My guess is he always considered our place his real home, but he never said that in so many words. Like I said, we Rasmussens keep things pretty close to the vest. The Lees, too, I guess.

"Yep, that's Mother to a 'T'," Bobby said, wiping tears of laughter out of his eyes.

Harlan and Bobby were wrong, though. In fact, I think we were all surprised by her little "prank." She'd never been much of a one for jokes or levity of any sort. She was the serious one to Dad's clown, the disciplinarian, the one who kept that boat on an even keel—or tried to, anyway. I loved my dad dearly, we all did. At sixty-one I can still feel the terrifying joy of riding him bronco-style, him down on all fours, my legs not long enough to span his back so that I could dig my heels in, get a grip, instead had to grab a double-handful of his hair and hold on for dear life as he bucked and snorted. I'd say I wanted to be like him except that even as I child I instinctively knew there's no point in wanting to be like God, not because it was presumptuous but because it was too far-fetched. I know that Ruby and Bobby felt that way, too. We all three grew up keeping a close eye out for signs of preferential treatment from our father, but—when he was at home, which wasn't too much because of his work—he had a way of making it seem like each one of us was his special concern. I don't know how he had any time left over for Mother.

Only Harlan didn't take to him even though it seemed to me that Dad went out of his way to make him feel like one of his own children. But Harlan's heart belonged to Mother, always, only Mother.

Mother demonstrated that Harlan was an equal member of the family by steadfastly refusing to treat him any better than she treated us. One of the hallowed scenes of family lore was the time Harlan—he was six or seven—sat at the kitchen table watching Mother ice a cake for a church social. She'd just finished, stood up straight with her hands on her hips, and said, "There!" when Harlan, probably as surprised as anyone, shot his hand out and swiped an index-finger full of icing. *Whack!* Mother cracked him so hard over the head with a long-handled wooden spoon that it snapped in half. Harlan dropped from the chair like a pole-axed steer. Mother ran around the table and screamed—at seeing her nephew lying on the floor with blood pouring from his scalp, we thought, but no, it was at seeing what the vandalized side of her cake looked like.

She would have had the SCAN folks on her today, no doubt, but if they'd come for her back then they would have had to fight their way through Harlan first. The attack did not diminish by a whit his love for his aunt, his only true Mother.

Once a few weeks ago, when we knew the end was coming, Ruby said to me, "I wonder who'll throw the biggest fit when she goes, Bobby or Harlan?"—Bobby included because although he idolized our father just as Ruby and I did, he was always a mama's boy at heart. (Crybaby, crybaby.) I thought Ruby's question odd because it implied I wasn't in the running for the "miss Mother" prize. Everybody thinks the first-born care only about themselves, and I have two or three ex-wives who'd probably agree, but I love my family.

After her little prank, Mother settled back into her ragged breathing, eyes closed. We stood there and watched, each thinking his own thoughts, or maybe all of us thinking the same thought: when will it come? Now, this instant? No. Then, now? Not wanting it but at the same time wanting it to be over with because we were tired, none of us spring chickens. At that moment, in fact, Harlan pulled over a chair and sat down because he had that bum hip from some accident at the carpet store where he worked. Then Mother's eyes opened again—or one, at least, the left one, the right one didn't seem to work anymore—and she took as close to a deep breath as she could manage and whispered, "Where's my Caddy?"

Lord, we whooped and howled in laughter, slapped each other on the back, exchanged high-fives.

If the Harlan and the cake icing bit was the one most often told about Mother, the Cadillac anecdote was our favorite Dad story. It wasn't necessary to give the whole account. All one of us had to do was come out with the line, "Say, where's my Caddy?"—especially at some pointedly inappropriate time, in church, for instance—in order to reduce us Rasmussens to helpless laughter.

Dad told it on himself. We were in the money at that time. I don't think we children were ever quite sure what Dad did for a living. As soon as we were able to get our tongue twisted around it, Mother taught us to say "entrepreneur" so we could tell anyone who asked what our father did. (Harlan could never manage it; "on top of manure" was as close as he could come.) Dad, on the other hand, always described himself as "a riverboat gambler, only there aren't near enough riverboats these days." We lived high on the hog sometimes, more often didn't. He must have been on a winning streak in his "Caddy days." We kids were all in our teens then. We lived in a house with wall-to-wall carpeting, which I thought meant you were wealthy, and dad had a parcel of land that he had big plans for, he assured us. One day he drove out to "the farm," as he called it, where he had a rented bulldozer waiting for him. Where he ever learned to operate one, I don't know, but he spent all day clearing that land, using the dozer to push brush and small trees down into this gully on the edge of the property. At the end of the day he climbed off the dozer and headed for his car to come home, but the car wasn't where he was sure he'd left it. "Say, where's my Caddy?" he swore he said aloud although there was nobody but the crows to hear him. Turns out he'd cleared that Caddy along with the mountain of brush it was buried under at the bottom of the gully.

No one found the story any funnier than Dad did, although the rest of us gave him a run for his money. Well, at least Ruby, Bobby, and I did. Mother just walked out of the room. She loved Dad, of course, but not that up-and-down life. She would have preferred that he get a nine-to-five job, be home for supper every night, and so on. But that wasn't dad. With all the divorces in the Rasmussen family, it's a miracle that Mother and Dad stuck it out so long, indeed, stuck it out until Dad died. I guess you make compromises, but then I'm really not the person to consult on stuff like that.

Come to think of it, Harlan was living with us again at that time. I don't remember him laughing. He probably followed Mother right out of the room.

Now, though, he laughed—or tried, at least. But I think it was less at the famous line than the fact that Mother—his dear Lou—still could form words at all.

The laughter would die down, and then one of us would say, "Where's my Caddy?" and it'd start up again. This went on for several minutes until Bobby said "Shh" and pointed to Mother. She seemed to be trying to talk, and we all leaned forward to listen. She said something that sounded like "glub glub." Her mouth was working like she was trying to swallow.

Then the nurse came in. She leaned over the bed and swept her palm gently over Mother's forehead.

"I think our Lou needs some clean sheets," she said. "Why don't you all go get some lunch while I take care of things in here."

The cafeteria was at the far end of a labyrinth of hallways where we used to lose ourselves in Mother's early days in the hospital, but now they were as familiar to us as our own homes. We'd barely reached the first turning when Ruby said, "It's too early for lunch. Besides, I need a smoke."

Harlan used to be a big smoker but gave it up after his wife died of emphysema, and Bobby and I had never taken it up. Still, we all dutifully followed Ruby outside.

Bucking the nationwide trend, the hospital had not yet totally banned smoking. Smokers, though, were restricted to an area about ten feet by ten on the parking lot to the left of the hospital entrance. The area was set off with saw horses and yellow crime-scene tape. It wasn't clear whether the provisional nature of the arrangement was a stopgap until something more permanent could be arranged or until smoking was banned altogether. Whichever, we filed through the "entrance"—an opening in the tape between two sawhorses—and stood shivering like the damned in the ninth circle of Hell. Or, as Harlan put it, "It's cold as a witch's tit out here."

"I feel like a hog in a holding pen just waiting to be slaughtered," Bobby said.

"I didn't ask you all to come out here with me," Ruby said. "Go to the cafeteria and stuff your fat faces."

Bobby, pudgy, glared but said nothing. Harlan just shrugged and grinned like, "That's our Ruby!"

And it was. The rest of us had brown (me) to shoe-polish-black (Bobby) hair, so it was a mystery where Ruby got the hair, freckles, and that almost transparent, bluish complexion of the redhead. "It's a recessive gene," Mother said, to which Dad replied, "Gene who?" "I didn't know the mailman's name was Gene," Ruby herself said. She would also joke that she got the red hair from Lonnie McPherson with the club foot and hare lip, poor guy, or, when she really wanted to get Mother's goat, from Reverend Dollar. (Mother was the only religious one in the family although Bobby went to church in his desperation to appear normal and respectable, to appear not to be a Rasmussen.)

Ruby could joke about her red hair, but anyone else who tried it had better protect his eyeballs. Ruby had a ferocious temper. Bobby was terrified of her—

but then Bobby was terrified of everything—and even Harlan, a tough little nut as the Lees tended to be, kept a respectful distance when the mood was on her. And the mood was often on her. Once after nobody had heard from her for a year or so, she showed up at Thanksgiving unannounced with a strange man on her arm. "Meet my new husband," she said. "What happened to the old husband?" we asked. "I killed him," she said. We were fairly sure she was joking.

Mother loved Bobby and Harlan dearly, and me, too, I'd like to think, but Ruby was her special care, as is the way with mothers and daughters, I guess. (I have a daughter by my second wife, but, sadly, we never hit it off. I really don't know much about her.) Mother had plenty to worry about with Ruby, a wild one from the cradle. But Mother was also the only one who could handle her. (Maybe Dad could have if he'd ever tried because Ruby adored him, but "handling" wasn't in his job description.) The way Mother handled Ruby when she got too far out of line was to grab her by the earlobe and pull her into the bedroom, saying, "Come on, kiddo, you and I need to have a talk." Ruby would return subdued, at least for awhile, and rubbing that ear.

I looked up at Ruby. She was puffing on her cigarette as if she were angry at it, and rubbing her earlobe. Reading my mind? Well, we were all remembering.

I shivered. It was a raw late-February day, and the blue sky occasionally flashing through the slush-gray clouds only made it seem colder.

Bobby looked miserable with his hands rammed deep into his greatcoat pockets and his hunched shoulders pushing his collar up around his ears. He was doing something with his lips, sort of pursing and unpursing them, like when he was a boy and was about to start bawling.

I never liked him—not his fault, but that doesn't change the fact. Some sort of Freudian thing involved, no doubt. I'd subconsciously resolved myself to a little sister's rivalry for Mother's affection, but I hadn't counted on another male entering the picture. That psycho-babble wouldn't have meant anything to me back then, of course. Back then I would've just said he was an irritating little namby-pamby crybaby and left it at that. Was the problem that I saw myself in him? Unlike pudgy little Bobby, I had our father's size but never his strength, bravery, or, I don't know, call it *joie de vive*. When I went from woman to woman and job to job, it wasn't because I was burning my candle at both ends but because when the going got tough, I got going. I wanted to run to Mother, but there'd be that fat little bastard on her lap. The ironic thing was that of all of us it'd been li'l Bobby who stood his ground, made it his life's work to stand his ground—one wife, one job for thirty years, kids and grandkids, a house with two fireplaces and an automatic lawn sprinkler system. Oh, I know, it's all in the name of keeping the terrors at bay, the tears at bay, but who's to say it hasn't worked better for him than whatever I've tried? Probably that's why I hate the little bastard so.

He was still doing that thing with his mouth. I finally figured out he wasn't trying not to cry but was working himself up to say something. Then he did:

"Say, where's my Caddy?"

A joke from that joyless little prick was even less to be expected than from our mother, so once again we laughed. And laughed. Ruby almost choked on her cigarette. She put her hand on my arm to steady herself as she *hack hack hacked*. (I was never afraid of her because, even though two years younger, she was always my protector, "Chuck's little mother," Dad called her. Once, our neighbor ran over and hammered on our door, hollering that a tornado was on the way, then ran off, not realizing Ruby and I were the only ones in the house. We were probably around six and eight at the time. We climbed under the big mission-oak table in the dining room, and there Ruby took me into her arms and patted my cheek and crooned, "It's all right, Chuckie boy, Chuckie boy, it's all right." I don't understand how she turned out to be such a hard woman. But then I don't understand how any of us turned out to be what we are.)

Bobby, who'd been laughing less than smirking proudly at the success of his joke, suddenly scowled and said to Harlan, "How come you're not laughing? What put the bug up your butt?"

I was shocked. Bobby was hardly the confrontational type, and if he were to take on anybody, it surely wouldn't be Harlan. They'd been the closest to each other in age, closer to each other in every way than they ever were to Ruby or me, even though they didn't seem to have much in common: Bobby the timorous little bookworm (not from any great intellectual fondness, I suspect, but because it was safer between those pages) and Harlan, quiet but a pit bull in a fight, more comfortable with his head under the hood of a car than with a book in his hands.

"I ain't got no critter up my butt, Bobby." Harlan said it gently, affectionately, trying to calm his old buddy down.

"Well, you've got something someplace. Why aren't you laughing?"

"Bobby," I cautioned, but he shot back, "Stay out of it, Chuck."

Well, that showed how far I'd sunk on the manhood scale if little Bobby Rasmussen was telling me to shut up. If it'd been Ruby who'd spoken to him, he would've crapped his size 40 drawers. Ruby, though, was just sucking with great concentration on her cigarette, not looking at anybody like she used to do when Mother and Dad got into it, like she was getting ready to disappear for another year or two

"Why aren't you laughing, Harlan?"

"I guess I just don't find that particular joke too funny."

"Yeah, well, what's wrong with 'that particular joke'?"

Harlan didn't say anything, and Bobby asked him again, and then Harlan said, "Because there never was no Caddy."

"What are you talking about? We all saw that Caddy. It was sky blue."

"Yeah, Harlan" I said, "I rode in that Caddy many times. We all did."

I looked at Ruby for confirmation, but she took that moment to flick away her cigarette butt and light up a new one. Harlan shook his head. "That's not what I meant. There was a Caddy all right, but that's not what happened to it. It didn't wind up at the bottom of no gully under no brush."

"Well, what happened to it, then?" I said.

He shook his head again, sadly this time like he wished he hadn't started this thing up. Whatever this thing was. Then he said, "Well hell, think about it. Do you think if that's what happened, Floyd would have just left that Caddy there?" Harlan said. Just as he called Mother "Lou," he called Dad "Floyd." Only he said Lou in such a way that it sounded like he was saying Mother, or maybe Mama. Floyd, though, sounded just like Floyd. "There wasn't no bulldozer out on that farm that day. I know because I was. Floyd dropped me off out there to cut weeds out of the fence while he drove over to Pinckney to visit his lady friend. They had some kind of run-in, and she took off in the Caddy. Didn't seem like he ever went to any effort to get his car back, so you can guess who was in the wrong on that deal. A guy at the Standard station in town gave him a lift back out to the farm and picked me up, brought us both home. You remember us coming back in the wrecker, don't you?"

I didn't, but that didn't mean anything. I would have been in my late teens then, and I didn't pay much attention to anything except my own private little world. Haven't really gotten over that, I guess.

"How did you know about a woman in Pinckney if you were out working on the farm?" I asked. "How did you know she took off with the Caddy?"

"Heard it. Everybody knew about Floyd and his women."

"Bullshit, bullshit," Bobby said, and kept right on saying it.

"How come you heard it but we didn't?" I said, and Harlan answered, "Because I didn't walk around with my eyes and ears closed like you people."

He said "you people" like he was spitting it. My God, what had he thought of us all those years? I thought we were his family, our home his home.

"Bullshit, bullshit," Bobby kept on like a skipping record player.

"Yeah, well, if you're so sure it's bullshit, why don't you go ask Lou?" Harlan said.

"You think I won't?" Bobby said like a little boy working himself up to accepting a dare.

Harlan frowned like he realized he'd gone too far. "Sure you would, Bobby. But let's forget it, OK? Forget I said anything."

"Oh no, you said it, so we're going to go see."

"Bobby, don't—"

But Bobby was already heading through the gap in the crime scene tape. Harlan called for him to stop, then headed after him. He put his hand on Bobby's arm, but Bobby threw it off, and they disappeared into the hospital.

I turned to Ruby and started to ask her if she thought it was true, but after one look at her face I said, "You knew it all along, didn't you?"

She shrugged. "Sure. Why do you think I hated her so much, letting that son of a bitch treat her that way."

I couldn't get words out. You wouldn't have been bothered so much if you hadn't loved her, I wanted to say. I wanted to say, You called Dad a son of a bitch, but I know you adored him. We all adored him. I wanted to ask how I could have understood so little about all of us, Rasmussens and Lees, every single one of us. There was too much I wanted to say, I couldn't say it all, I couldn't say anything.

We stood there. A black man in green scrubs came out of the hospital and started to enter the smoking area but took one look at us and turned around and went the other way.

We stood there long enough that Ruby finished her cigarette and lit up another. Then Bobby and Harlan came out of the hospital and headed toward us, and Ruby took the cigarette out of her mouth and dropped it on the pavement like she was through with smoking now.

"Well," Harlan said, "Lou's gone."

Then he started to cry, and at the same time Bobby screwed his knuckles into his eyes like he did as a child right before sending up a despairing wail. Ruby picked up her cigarette from the pavement, flicked at it a couple of times with her fingernail, then put it in her mouth and took a long puff. A tear fell off the end of her nose and hit the cigarette dead center. Ruby took the cigarette out of her mouth and gaped at it with a look of absolute horror.

Bobby and Harlan were standing on the other side of the tape. I led them through the opening. I was the oldest, taking charge. Now we were all together. I'd give us a few minutes to grieve, each in his own way, and then I'd lead us back into the hospital, down that labyrinth of halls to her room where she'd be waiting patiently for us, and I'd cry out, *Mother, Mom, Mama, here's your family.*

Afterglow

When you meet somebody and wind up liking them better than you thought you would, it's enough to make you wonder if that ol' glass isn't half full after all. It doesn't happen often, though, and when it does you should cherish it—if *cherish* isn't too corny a word to use. Now, why did I say that? I'm trying to be a person who can use a word like *cherish* without blushing, who can be sensitive and caring of others, because the kind of guy I've been up to now hasn't worked out too well for me. It's tough going, though.

It was a year ago today, July 4th, that I met Trent Ulmer. His wife, Dixie, worked at the Med Center with a lady I was seeing at the time, Gabrielle. Don't recall her last name. We were going to have a barbecue at Gabrielle's condo out on Highway 10. She didn't break the news to me that she'd invited another couple until I was sitting there drinking my first beer, too late to bail out. Looking back, I think we were probably already on the downhill slide, and springing this other couple on me was Gabrielle's way of letting me know she didn't want to be alone with me. Maybe I'm wrong. That glass has always seemed half empty to me. Like I said, I'm fighting the dark side, but that dark side keeps fighting back.

Gabrielle could tell I wasn't crazy about the idea of having to socialize with complete strangers, but she told me I'd like the guy, Trent, a college professor. College professor!

"A prof, huh? Hot dang, got hisself a whole bunch of that ejumacation, I bet."

As soon as I said it I knew I'd sounded like some redneck horse's ass. Well, it's true, my neck does get pretty red in my business, putting in new sidewalks and driveways for folks. I'm the owner, but I spend half my time out under the sun with the boys. I don't apologize for my job. I like pouring concrete. You get finished and it's all right there in front of you, good job or bad, you know it right away. No questions asked. If you work with people, now, you run into complications, a thing I don't like.

Anyway, because I was embarrassed at sounding like a jerk, I tried my best to be friendly when the other couple showed up. Turns out it wasn't hard at all.

The first thing Trent said after the introductions was, "Is this any way to treat a guest, Randal? I've been here close to twenty seconds already and I don't see a single beer in my hand."

How could you be uncomfortable with a guy like that? We killed a solid hour just talking about beer. He'd spent a few years in the Army—an officer, but I tried not to hold that against him. I never made it past Airman First Class and spent my entire tour in North Dakota first, then Alaska, then Greenland. I tell people I was in the Ice Force. Trent, though, was in Europe, Asia, all over, and had drunk beer in a lot of different countries, a thing I liked to hear about. I told him that if he'd promise to just lecture on beer, I'd take one of his courses.

When we finished talking about beer, we turned to sports. Turns out Trent liked sports, too, so we were set.

The girls were in the kitchen, didn't seem to be bothered by us pretty much ignoring them. Probably should have taken that as another sign about where Gabrielle and I were headed. Nowhere.

I really don't remember much at all about Dixie that first day. Blonde, short but built. Not that I thought about the built part. When I'd hear a guy say the way he wanted to go was getting shot by a jealous husband, I'd say, "Welcome to it. I don't want to get shot by anybody for anything." Now, though, I don't know. I'd like to see that woman worth taking a bullet for. What worries me is that maybe I already have and didn't know it.

The girls finished cooking, and we ate out on the balcony because we thought we might be able to see the fireworks display over in Maumelle. No such luck. It was hot out there, so the girls went back inside, and Trent and I started talking about fireworks. Trent was about my age, mid-thirties, and we sounded like a couple of old farts talking about the good ol' days when we'd spend all day shooting off firecrackers, getting in bottle-rocket fights and such.

"I remember when we were kids you couldn't legally buy fireworks inside the Little Rock city limits," Trent said. "Today, though, you can't even buy them in Pulaski County."

"Not even in the county?"

"Not in the whole goddamn county."

"That's un-American."

I told him I knew for a fact you could still buy them in Saline County because we'd done a job in Benton last week and I'd passed a half-dozen stands on the way.

"Let's go buy some," Trent said.

"What, right now?"

I said it'd be at least a half hour there and back, and he said we should be able to get another beer drunk in that time. *I love this guy!* I said to myself.

"What about the women?" I said.

"The women? What are we, men or mice?"

We drove down to Saline County and bought firecrackers and rockets and Roman candles and didn't even go back into the condo to say hi to the girls when we got back but shot everything off on the condo parking lot, keeping an eye out for the cops.

I won't lie, it was a pretty emotional experience for me because I started thinking about my dad. Every 4th we'd shoot fireworks off at night after my dad got home from work. My mom died when I was a little kid. I almost think I can remember her, but I may just be remembering my dad talking about her. Everybody always feels sorry for the kid in a situation like that, but I always felt sorriest for my dad. He was the one who carried her in his heart. He died when I was in the Air Force in North Dakota. They let me come home for his funeral.

When Trent and I went back inside, I expected to catch hell from Gabrielle for being gone so long, but she didn't bat an eye. Yeah, yeah, another sign I should have picked up on, but I wasn't as sensitive then as I am now.

I checked out Dixie next. I figured she'd be giving poor ol' Trent a dirty look. She was giving him a look, all right, but not a dirty one. It took me a long time to figure out what kind of look it was.

I saw Gabrielle less and less after that. Not sure exactly why. I regret it now because she was a terrific lady, pretty as her name, smart, funny. Probably she wanted more of a commitment than I was ready to make. I was thirty-five then, and it seemed like the world was full of women just as hot as Gabrielle. Lose one, go down to Cajun's or Smitty's on Friday night and pick out another one, no problemo. Now I'm thirty-six and feel like I'm on the downhill side. I spend less time thinking about the new thing on Friday night and more time thinking about what I've lost out on. That list is pretty long.

Anyway, at the same time I was seeing less of Gabrielle, I started seeing more of Trent. It started with Trent calling me about doing lunch because he'd heard from Gabrielle, I guess, that I had a job laying new sidewalks at that little strip mall across from the university. We ate at a Mexican place over there, me in my work clothes and sweat. I figured Trent'd be in a corduroy jacket with leather elbow patches and smoking a pipe—college professor—but he was dressed about like me, minus the sweat. We talked about Mexican food and sports, and the topic turned to golf. I'm a golf nut. I play a couple of times a week, more if things are slow on the job. Use Ping irons and Callaway woods, currently back to Titleist Pro-V1s after trying Nike balls for a year. Like I said, a golf nut. Trent said he was so bad even duffers kept their distance so he wouldn't contaminate their swings. I said let's play sometime, just to be polite, because he's right, it can mess up your game to play with somebody really godawful. Well, he was so bad that godawful wouldn't have wanted to play with him, either, but he was so good-natured about it, I enjoyed myself. We started playing about once a week.

As much as anything, I liked it when the golf was over with and we'd have a beer or two on the 19th hole and shoot the breeze. Just a couple of guys.

One day he asked me how things were going with Gabrielle, and I said there wasn't much going on there at all. He said he knew the feeling because that's about how they were going with Dixie. I told him I was sorry to hear that and asked him if they were separated or something. He said no, he didn't mean that but, well, it was a hard thing for one man to talk to another man about.

For a crazy moment I thought he was going to tell me he was gay and had the hots for me, that the whole business—going out for fireworks, lunch, the golf—was all part of a plan to get close to me. But that, thank God, wasn't it. No, his problem was he hadn't been doing any good in the sack.

"I haven't been able to do a thing since I got back from Iraq," he said.

Jesus. I knew he'd spent several years in the Army, had been all over, but I didn't even remember him saying he'd been in Iraq. When was that, anyway? I recalled him talking about "last year" at the university, so he'd been in Little Rock at least a year going on two. It'd been that long since he'd had sex with his wife?

"Were you . . . injured over there?" I asked. It was none of my business, but then he'd brought it up.

"No. But I saw things over there . . . did things. . . . There's a lot of guilt. I haven't been any good for Dixie since I got back."

"Jesus. Have you seen anybody about it?"

"You mean a shrink? No, I don't have a lot of faith in the talking cure. I saw what I saw. I did what I did. Talking isn't going to change a thing."

I didn't know what he meant by that "talking cure" stuff. Probably some college professor shit.

"Well, at least you talked to Dixie."

"No. Dixie is the one person I couldn't possibly talk to about it."

"Trent, she's your *wife*."

"Well, I haven't been much of a husband."

"That exactly why you have to talk to her, man. Explain."

He shook his head. "Can't possibly do it."

⁂

It was my idea to go talk to Dixie. Trent for sure didn't suggest it and I don't think even hinted it, but I'll say this: at the time I didn't think I was doing anything Trent would have objected to.

I remembered Trent saying that Dixie only worked half days now, mornings, so I figured there was a good chance I'd catch her at home in the afternoon. I was kind of hoping I'd miss her. I was nervous as hell. I'd never done anything like this before, this mission of mercy thing. At the same time it felt kind of good thinking about somebody other than myself for a change, so I forced myself to go through with it.

Well, she was home, all right. As soon as she came to the door, I just came out with it. Told her I wanted to talk to her about Trent, that he was a pretty unhappy guy, which would be no news flash to her, but there were things she didn't know.

She nodded like she'd been expecting something like this and said, "Maybe we could go get a cup of coffee." She went back into the house to make a call, and then we drove over to this coffee house, Java Jive, in the Heights

At Java Jive, Dixie drank tea made out of flowers and I drank a three-dollar cup of coffee, black. I cut to the chase. "Dixie, Trent's real unhappy. I know I don't have to tell you that. I feel bad about it because I think he's a great guy and—"

"Then maybe you should go live with him. It's not all a merry-go-round for me, either."

"I know that, Dixie. I know the problem he's been having. You know what I mean. Look, I'm the last one to be giving advice, but—"

"How are things with Gabrielle these days, Randal?"

I winced. "Not so good, Dixie, not so good."

"What happened there, Randal?"

"To be honest with you, Dixie, I'm not really sure."

"That's the sort of thing you should know, Randal."

She really threw me on that one. There are things that are true, and then there are things that are so true they knock the wind out of you. Why didn't I know what went wrong between Gabrielle and me? But I wasn't there to talk about me. I forced the conversation back to Trent.

"You're right, Dixie. The funny thing is right now I know more about your problem, yours and Trent's, than I do about mine."

"Ah. You know all about us. How nice."

I'd sweated less pouring concrete in July.

"I know Trent's problem is that he feels guilty, that he saw things and did things he can't get over, can't quit thinking about, and it's causing his other problems. You know what I'm talking about. Physical problems. Sexual. You know."

Dixie just smiled. She seemed to be enjoying this a lot more than I was.

"Things he saw and did. What things, exactly?"

"He didn't get specific. I was in the Air Force when the first Iraqi thing was going on, but I didn't get any closer than Greenland. I was a civilian by the time this latest shit started up. But I've seen news clips and read a little about it. I can use my imagination. Trent must have got into some terrible shit over there."

"Iraq? Randal," Dixie said with a smile that looked like it was carved out of ice with a scalpel, "Trent never got closer to Iraq than Kaiserslautern, Germany. That's where we met."

I was trying to think of what say, think of what to *think*, when she looked at her watch and said, "Come on. Time to go."

I pulled up to the curb in front of her house and waited for her to get out, but she said, "Come in, Randal. There's something I want to show you."

I followed her in. Instead of turning toward the den, she led us the other way. I followed her into a bedroom.

"Here's where it all happens . . . or doesn't happen," she said.

She sat down on the edge of the bed.

"Dixie, I think I'd better be going," I said.

She held her hand out to me. "Come on," she said. "Come on . . . Come on . . . Come on . . ."

I'm six-one by two-hundred and pump iron four times a week down at Gold's, but I'm a weak man. I took her hand.

I'd go over there at 2:30 every Monday, Wednesday, and Friday afternoon. She said Trent had classes then.

I wasn't proud of what I did. The only thing I'll give myself credit for is that I never tried to justify or rationalize it, didn't say, Well, I was only doing what Trent wasn't man enough to do, or, Dixie wanted it as bad as I did, or, She came on to me first. I knew it was wrong and went ahead and did it, three times a week, 2:30 in the afternoon.

Yeah, I felt bad about Trent, bad enough that I couldn't face him anymore, but I won't lie, I got a thrill out of doing it with another man's wife. She got a thrill out of it, too, kind of kinky at that. We always had to do it on Trent's side of the bed. Her idea. If I tried to draw her over to the other side, she'd pull away and say, "No, over here." The only time we did it anywhere else was one time, well, they had this chest, I'd call it a cedar chest, along the wall on Trent's side of the bed. Well, I'll leave the rest to your imagination.

It went on for months. Went on longer than Gabrielle and I were together. I've tried to remember if I was ever with a woman longer than I banged Dixie.

Ouch. I shouldn't have said that. I don't want to make it sound dirty because it wasn't, at least not all of it and not the most important part, for me anyway. The neatest thing was that I'd started out thinking that Dixie was a cold bitch and that we both were just out to take what we wanted, but I discovered that she was a really sweet person, sensitive. I'd like to think that she'd changed her mind about me, too. In fact, I'm sure she did. In the beginning I'd no sooner get through the door than she'd take me by the hand and pull me into the bedroom, and let the good times roll. After a few months, though, we'd talk a little, ask each other about our days and so forth. She even began to make us a cup of tea. I'd never drunk tea in my life except once in a while iced, but I became a real fan of that Earl Grey. Dixie liked the herbal stuff. She tried to get me to drink it, but I told her it wasn't my cup of tea, ha ha. I wouldn't tell this to a bunch of guys over beers, but the truth is there were afternoons I would have taken a second cup of tea and skipped the bedroom. But after a little chit-chat and tea, Dixie would always start to get a little, oh, I don't know, antsy or something, would look at her watch and then jump up and grab my hand and say, "Come on."

Was I falling in love with her? I think I was really attracted to the idea of falling in love with her. Is that the same thing? I guess that's another thing I need to figure out.

The affair or whatever you want to call it ended about a month ago, on June 7th.

What happened that afternoon came as a big shock to me—the shock of my life, no question—but I shouldn't have been so surprised. The signs, the clues were there. Like glancing through the university course schedule someone had left on the table at Supercuts and finding that all the classes Trent was listed as teaching were in the mornings. And one time turning the opposite way I usually did out of the cul-de-sac they lived on, trying to take a shortcut to the Home Depot on Chenal, and seeing a car just like Trent's parked about a block away. I didn't give either one of them a second thought, though. I wasn't the suspicious type, maybe because there'd never been anybody I cared about enough to get suspicious over.

OK, no more dragging this out. You've already guessed the punch line to this traveling salesman joke, you're already snickering. Probably I would be too if it'd been somebody else it happened to and I heard about it down a Smitty's. *You're shittin' me, man. What a hoot!* But I don't think there's anything funny about it.

We were in bed—or I should say on the bed. Just getting going good when I heard something in the closet. I stopped what I was doing and said, "What was that?" Dixie said it was just something falling in the closet. She kept her hair dryer on a hook in the closet, and sometimes it'd fall. But it didn't sound like a hairdryer falling to me.

I looked at the closet, the part I could see. Their master bedroom was set up funny. On the south side, at the foot of the bed, a wall ran three-quarters of the way across the room. On the other side of this wall was a vanity and double-sink and beyond that the full south wall with closets behind folding doors running its entire length. All the doors had louvered panels in them. The last door was the only one that could be seen from the bed—Trent's side of the bed. I'd always wondered why they hadn't replaced the missing louver in that door. It left a gap of about half an inch. I stared at the gap.

"It was just the hair dryer falling," Dixie said. "Things fall. Come on. . . . Come on."

I got the hell out of there.

I've had a tough month since then. I tried to just forget about it, but that didn't work. Then I thought I'd make a joke of the whole thing. Along about then we finished up a parking lot job at that new pizza restaurant down on Rebsamen—my first shot at asphalt work—and to celebrate I had the crew out to a picnic at Allsoop Park, beer and grilled steaks. I told them the whole story, and they laughed and hooted all right, said, "You da man!" and "You dog, you," stuff like that. The only one not laughing was me.

I wasn't mad at Trent and Dixie, not even if they'd rigged the whole thing from the beginning, drew me in like a spider into a web. Wait, that's not right. Oh well, maybe it is. Maybe it was one spider getting drawn in by two other spiders. Aw, I don't know. I just feel sorry for them. Me, too. I think people want love so much they lose their way searching for it. For a while there I was lost right along with them. There are times I wish I still was.

You know what I miss most? I miss drinking tea with Dixie. I'd drink my Earl Grey, and she'd drink her herbal tea, and later in the bedroom I'd taste it on her lips, that first kiss, and I'd pretend it wasn't the first kiss before sex but the last kiss of the day, at night in bed, *Goodnight, Sweetheart,* and the next morning we'd get up and have breakfast, Corn Flakes and orange juice, and we'd tell each other to have a good day at work and be careful driving and, *Oh, by the way, I may be a little late this afternoon because me and my buddy Trent are going to try to get in nine at Hindman.* What a beautiful life that would have been.

They're the first people in my life I've missed in a long time, since my father, I guess. I remember the 4th of July when I was a kid, shooting off firecrackers and bottle rockets and cherry bombs during the day, and then my dad would come home tired from work but never too tired to take me out on the street after dark, and he'd set off fountains, I think they were called, these cones that'd shoot up fountains of sparks. Roman candles, too. He'd tell me to stand back because fireworks were dangerous even though I'd been blowing up gallon paint cans and stuff with cherry bombs before he got home. But I'd do what he said because even then I knew it was a good thing to have someone who cared about you.

The only thing he'd let me do when I was a kid was hold sparklers. It'd be the last thing we'd do before we went back in. He'd light the sparklers, and we'd each hold one and holler, "Happy birthday, USA!"

"Let's spell it out," my dad would always say, and he'd spell out U-S-A against the night sky. I'd sing out "USA," too, but what I'd really spell was "Mama" and "Daddy" and then later, when I started to notice the girls, the name of whichever girl I currently had a crush on. I'd close my eyes and for the briefest moment see the letters still glowing brightly before they faded. It was so beautiful. Things are the most beautiful, I guess, right before they fade.

THE PATEK PHILLIPE

I've moved thirteen times in my young life that I can remember for a fact, the last four since our old man died and it's just been me and my brother Casey. (Our old lady vacated the premises about the time I learned to walk.) Our present landlord isn't as choosy as some about the rent being paid, so we've lived here at the Ozark Terrace Apartments over a year. There's a leak in the ceiling in our bathroom, and I think one of these days we're going to be paid an unannounced visit by the guy above us, seated on a toilet. There's a leak under the kitchen sink, too, and no screens on the windows and roaches we can't get rid of despite the Raid bomb we set off and about asphyxiated ourselves. The air-conditioner works, though, and in Arkansas if the AC works, everything else is gravy. Also on the plus side until he up and died was Shorty Howell, who lived in the house next door. Shorty owned a Patek Phillipe.

In case you don't know, a Patek Phillipe is a watch, very high class, very expensive, like a Rolex only more so. Shorty never wore it, but he'd take it out of his pocket and show it to you at the drop of a hat.

"Here, let me show you something. What do you think of this?" was about the second thing out of his mouth the first time we met. Then he hauled out the watch.

At the time we were sitting on lawn chairs on our "patio," we called it, which had originally been a driveway. The Ozark Terrace Apartments are really just a long cinder block affair, five units up and five down. We live in the last one, down, a driveway coming off of Sixth Street going right by our end and leading to the parking lot and another drive coming off of Ozark Street on the other end. That was one more drive than the place needed, Casey figured, so the day after we moved in, he blocked off "our" drive with a couple of sawhorses he stole from a construction site and some of that yellow crime scene tape. If the landlord or anyone else ever had a complaint about it, they never told us. Maybe they figured it was best not to. They would be right.

Anyway, we were out there on our lawn chairs enjoying a beer or three when this old coot comes over from this grubby little house next door that looks like the kind of place they would have torn down to build our two-bit apartment house and considered it an improvement. I figured he'd come over to bitch at us, but instead he eyes the sawhorses admiringly and says, "Damn. Wish I'd thought of that."

That was the first thing he said. The second was, "Here, let me show you something. What do you think of this?" And out comes the watch.

This was sure-fire evidence he didn't know who we were because people who know us tend to keep their valuables out of sight. We're Ingrams. Almost never Casey and Scott but "the Ingram brothers" or more often "them Ingrams" in the grammar-challenged way folks likely to know us would talk. I, on the other hand, am in college as we speak . (Did you catch that "on the other hand"? No Ingram in the history of the world until me has ever said, "On the other hand." Me, though—"on the other hand," "whereas," "moreover"—I can really sling it when I want to.)

"That there is a Patek Phillipe. Patek Phillipe," Shorty repeated, then spelled it. "Go ahead, hold it," he said, handing it to Casey, who evidently—"evidently," did you get that? "evidently"!—was so startled by the man's naivety that he didn't immediately assume the sprint position and head off to the high timber, watch in tow. "Yeah, now pass it on to the other feller so he can touch it. Don't put it on your wrist, though. The sweat on your wrist would just eat that baby up. That baby's 18-carat gold, and 18-carat gold has no greater enemy than the human sweat gland. Go on, feel how light that baby is. Now give it back here."

It was light, it felt like nothing in my hand. You could tell it was pure class all the way. I handed it back, to Casey, though, not Shorty, and Casey hefted it in his palm, and his left eye closed about three-quarters sort of speculatively like he was measuring the watch against some idea he had in his mind, and I knew what that idea was. But Casey handed it back to Shorty.

"Now what do you call that again?" Casey asked.

"A Patek Phillipe. Swiss-made, of course. That there is what you call a Perpetual Calendar, 18-carat gold. That model brand new will set you back sixteen thousand dollars. This here one is probably twenty years old, but I figure I could get nine, ten thousand for it without having to Jew anybody at all on it."

"Where'd you get it?" Casey asked, and Shorty said, "That's for me to know and you to find out."

Now that sounded borderline smart-alecky to me, but Casey just laughed and said, "How much did you say that thing is worth again?" And Shorty said, "Eight, nine, ten thousand, easy. If you don't believe me, look it up on that internet."

Yeah, like Shorty Howell would know anything about the internet. He was I'd guess right about eighty years old, leathery skin and stooped and big gnarled hands for a little guy like he'd done a lot of hard work out in the sun, a farmer or brick-layer or something. I had trouble seeing ol' Shorty booting up.

Me, now, I'm not just computer literate, I'm computer *savvy*. One of my first courses at the junior college was Practical Computer Applications, and today I can whip up some PowerPoint or Excel or what have you without half thinking about it. I don't go to the JC every day because it's a thirty-minute drive with the blood-sucking oil companies jacking gas prices up and all, but I go in for classes every Monday Wednesday Friday, and the first thing I do once I hit campus is commandeer a computer in the library and check my email. I've never received an email except for official stuff from the college and spam and shit like that because nobody I know owns a computer, but you have to keep checking. You have to stay prepared.

Anyway, the first day on the ol' HP after talking to Casey, I Googled Patek

Phillipe, and although it's hard to be too definite about anything because I didn't know exactly how old the watch was or the exact model, damned if it didn't look like Shorty wasn't just shoveling smoke about his little baby being worth several thou.

I held off on telling Casey, though. Casey's an odd one, and you can't always tell what he'll do in a given situation, but if he happened to be in what I think of as "an Ingram mood," he'd just run right out the door, do a one-and-a-half through Shorty's front window and rip that watch out of Shorty's pants pocket using only his front teeth. That's been the Ingram way, but that doesn't mean it always has to be the Ingram way. The Ingram way pretty much has always meant some wild times followed by incarceration and then death by alcoholism, lung cancer, or gunshot. I prefer to see a career in my future. That's why I'm going to the JC, one more semester there then on to the university in Fayetteville, then a degree and I can name my price. It'll all take money, though, and I'm enough of an Ingram to keep all options open.

We lived across the patio from Shorty for almost a year before he died—and no, we didn't have any hand in that. Us Ingrams will do just about anything, I grant you that, but we draw the line at premeditated murder except for Uncle Dale's branch of the family, and we don't like to claim them. We didn't see Shorty every day quite, but close to it. He bought an aluminum lawn chair at Wal-Mart just so he could sit with us on the patio. In bad weather or when the mosquitoes were too ornery, we'd sit in our place and chew the fat and lift a few, or we'd go to his house. More our place, though, because believe it or not our place looked pretty good compared to that dump of Shorty's. I don't know what he did for money—Social Security, I guess, and not much else because the old boy was poor as a church mouse. In the living room he had an eleven-inch, black and white portable TV, rabbit ears, sitting on an upended, plastic bucket, two rickety, high-backed wooden chairs, and a tassel-shaded floor lamp that looked like it'd been looted from some French whorehouse. Smelled like it, too. The whole place smelled like houses do that have nothing but some old person living in them. Smelled like something was about to die there, which it was.

Shorty himself didn't smell bad, though. He always smelled like Ivory Soap to me and had every hair in place and clothes ironed, always a crease in his pants, even in his jeans. He ironed his clothes himself. I know he did because we found an iron in there when we came over to ransack the place after he died. No ironing board though. He must have ironed on the card table in the kitchen because that was the only table in the house. That's where he ate, too, sitting in the aluminum lawn chair he'd drag out to the patio when he visited us out there. He'd bring it into the living room when we came for a visit, too, because he only had two old wooden chairs besides that. "Come on, sit, sit," he'd say to Casey and me, almost begging one of us to take the aluminum chair like a good host who's offering the guest the best chair in the house, which it for sure was. Those wooden chairs were hard. They'd give you the ass ache in about twelve seconds.

The kitchen didn't have anything else in it except a washing machine that'd about dance across the floor when it was running because Shorty could never get the thing balanced right, and the bathroom had nothing but a tub and an old Army duffle bag that he used for dirty clothes, I guess, and his bedroom had a one-man cot with a mattress about half an inch thick and a chest of drawers and a stack of cardboard boxes in one corner and more in the closet with nothing of value in any of them. Believe me, we looked.

I'm telling you that boy was poor.

Which brings us back to the Patek Phillipe. Where'd he get it? He'd been in the Army in World War Two and afterwards did a little bit of everything, according to Shorty, but as far as I could tell, "everything" pretty much boiled down to janitoring. Nothing wrong with janitoring, but I never saw a janitor with two nickels to rub together. So I figured the simplest explanation was that Shorty stole the watch, but Casey thought that he wasn't the type.

"Hell, anybody'll steal if you leave it laying around in front of them," I said.

"No. Not Shorty."

Casey didn't want to hear any talk about Shorty stealing that watch. Why he'd get so bent out of shape about it I don't know. His whole attitude toward the watch, toward Shorty, was something I could never quite get a handle on. But then Casey wasn't your typical Ingram.

Now, if it'd been our old man in the deal instead of Casey, that watch would have been out of Shorty's hands before the sun set on another day. Our old man or any of our uncles or cousins except Rex the preacher, and he might have been running the biggest scam of all. Uncle Dale and our cousin Damon would have had that watch about two seconds after Shorty flashed it that first time, and if Shorty would have put up a fuss they would have just bashed his head in. Think I'm kidding? Check out their press clippings. Me and my old man would have had it, too, but we wouldn't have done a homicide for it. No, my old man wasn't one of the mean Ingrams, just one of the dumb ones. He would have kicked in a window in Shorty's house one night without even checking to see if anyone was inside, and then the law would have caught him climbing back out, watch in hand, and then he'd be in jail again. He spent more time in jail than out, best I can remember, but he died out, of lung cancer, a smoker. His last bit of orneriness was when he was in the hospital, dying in one of those clear plastic oxygen tent things, and he got in a fight with a nurse because they wouldn't let him smoke in there and, weak as he was from dying, they had to call hospital security to get him under control. Like I said, dumb.

Anyway, I finally told Casey that the watch was legit, and, our family tree being the twisted son of a bitch it is, I figured we'd have that Patek Phillipe sooner rather than later, the only delay being Casey trying to figure out how to get 'er done without us having to move again out of the deal. We might not be lucky enough to get a patio the next place.

I spent weeks waiting for Casey to come up with a plan for getting that watch before I finally figured out he didn't want to get that watch. I have several theories about that, but the simplest explanation is that Casey genuinely liked ol' Shorty. Now, Ingrams like people like anyone else. Ingrams have friends. But we never let friendship get in the way of a business opportunity. I mean let's face it, they are a lot more eighty year old buzzards out there than there are Patek Phillipes, am I right? That's how an Ingram would see it, anyway. Problem is, Casey just never was a typical Ingram.

Casey is five years older than me, but if you'd subtract the time he spent in the system—Casey says every day you spend in the lockup is a day you never lived—that makes us about the same age. Or at least that's what I say just to get his goat. The truth is that Casey even as a kid was like a little old man—or maybe I should say like a little old woman. I had a father but never had a mother that I knew anything about, so Casey was pretty much it. He the same as raised me, even when our old man was on the inside and we were shunted off to Aunt Caroline and Uncle Troy's, it was Casey who saw to it that I washed and ate enough and had on enough clothes on winter days.

I led him a merry chase sometimes. Casey had been scared of trains from even before I knew him, and one of my favorite tricks was to stand on the railroad tracks when a train was coming, and Casey would just bawl and bawl and beg me to come down off those tracks. One day he screamed so hard he broke a blood vessel or something in his throat and blood came shooting out his mouth, so I didn't do that any more, but I'd threaten him with it when he'd do something to piss me off like nagging me to wash my ears.

Now, I'm not saying that Casey was a wimp or anything. No, he was a tough son of a bitch when he wanted to be, bigger than me, he could have whipped me with one hand but he never did. He spent quite a bit of time in the juvenile lockup for this and that and then did three years for beating a guy just about to death over a girl. Our old man just couldn't understand it. He could see risking jail time to steal some money or maybe hijack a truck load of cigarettes or something, but a *girl*? "Jesus H., Casey, you don't risk your life fighting some guy over no goddamn girl! Use your head! Some girl messes with you, you rape the shit out of her, that's fine, but fight some guy who's probably packing heat? Now you're going to the Cummins unit and I'm stuck taking care of this goddamn kid all by myself."

This goddamn kid being me, obviously. I guess that's why when Casey got paroled three years later he told me two things: that he was through with women—they weren't worth the trouble—and he was going to take care of me so I'd never have to be in a foster home again. You see I'd spent a year in a foster home because our old man died two years into Casey's sentence, and Aunt Caroline and Uncle Troy wouldn't take responsibility for me because I'd been having my own problems with the law. I didn't really mind the foster home all that much, but Casey felt awful bad about it. Shows what guilt will do to a man. That's why I try not to have anything to do with it.

Anyway, I was seventeen when Casey got out of prison, and we've lived together ever since, moving four times. I like this last place best, the one with the patio, although I know it's a worry to Casey trying to get the rent paid maybe one month out of three and put food on the table and put me through college because the Pell grants don't pay everything, not even in JC, and with me wanting to go to the university next year—and Casey wanting it for me even more than I want it for myself, I think—it's a worry to him. That's why I just couldn't figure why Casey wouldn't steal that Patek Phillipe. Friendship just didn't seem to be enough of a reason, not even for Casey.

Here's my theory as to why Casey acted so strange around Shorty: he saw him as a father figure. I'd lay some Freud on you here except I missed that day in General Psych to go to the horse races in Hot Springs. Of course we'd had a real father, but he wasn't any better at that than he was at anything else except being a deadbeat, and there he was world class. Shorty, though, was a good old boy who'd share his beer with you and offer to fry you up a baloney sandwich, and most of all he always seemed glad to see you, which is something a fellow could get used to. Casey got used to it.

He got to where he spent most of his spare time with Shorty, not that he had much of that because he worked thirty-five hours a week at the Dollar Shop (they wouldn't give him forty or they'd have to pay benefits) and then washed dishes weekends at the Hacienda Mexican food joint. I told Casey to quit worrying about the goddamn tuition at the university. Something will come up, I said. It always does for me, being the lucky type. And if it doesn't, I'm not as bashful about making my own luck as Casey seems to have gotten lately. Sometimes I wonder if they didn't get the babies mixed up in the hospital when he was born.

I think that was another reason Casey spent so much time with Shorty: It was a helluva cheap date, Shorty generally furnishing the beer. I got damn bored with it, though.

A twenty-year-old red-blooded American male has to have more of a social life than swapping lies with an eighty-year-old, even if he is buying the beer. Weekend would come, and I'd be out on the town, leaving Casey and Shorty to it. Hard to have too wild a time, though, when the money runs out about the time the stars come out. Fanny Hickman, now, she would have kept me occupied a good while, but Casey messed that one up for me, at least I suspect it was Casey, and if I'm right, it was the oddest thing yet from an Ingram.

Here's what happened. Fanny and her husband Rudd Hickman lived on the upper floor of the apartment house, three from this end. For some reason they started visiting us out on the patio. It wasn't like they got a round of applause when they showed up. Shorty said that both of them together weren't worth a dry fart. He never said what he had against them, but I think it was because they didn't show the proper enthusiasm for Shorty's Patek Phillipe. Rudd allowed as to how it was probably a knock-off, and Fanny said she liked the Rolex that could go two-hundred feet under water. You can see how that would get them up near the top of Shorty's shit list. Casey didn't say anything about Fanny, but he didn't have any use for Rudd. He said Rudd was a doper and you couldn't trust dopers, which I thought was a pretty funny thing for an Ingram to say if you want to know the truth.

I didn't have anything against Rudd even if he was a doper. Hey, it's always 4:20 someplace in the world. And I liked Fanny a *lot*. She'd come down to the patio barefooted, wearing shorts and generally a halter top and no bra. I got the impression she didn't much like wearing clothes period, and once I got that notion in my head it was hard to think of anything else.

Fanny was a doper, too, only she hadn't been at it as long as Rudd and didn't look as strung out. They had a meth lab in their apartment although Rudd made it a point to do his deals somewhere else. A real professional. When he was off on business, I'd go up and visit Fanny, and we'd do our thing. She would turn you any way but loose, I kid you not.

Things were going fine until I happened to mention to Casey about the meth lab, and he asked me how I knew about it, and I said I'd seen it plenty of times when I was up there putting the wood to Fanny. That's when Casey blew his stack. At first I thought it was the meth lab that bothered him, but no, it was me messing around with a married woman. Didn't I know that was a good way to get myself killed? Then I remembered Casey doing time for about killing that guy over a woman, and our old man letting him have it for being so stupid, and Casey saying that was it for him and women. So I sort of understood where he was coming from, but that didn't mean I had to like it, and I told Casey to mind his own goddamn business and that I didn't need a goddamn nursemaid.

Casey didn't say anything to that, but the next day the law raided their apartment and hauled off Rudd and Fanny in handcuffs. I don't know for a fact that Casey called the police on them—and if he did it would sure as hell be a first for an Ingram—but let's just say the circumstantial evidence points to dear old bro. I was heap big pissed. Fanny was the best piece of ass I'd had in a long time. And her being married already, she wouldn't be coming after me to marry her or for child support if she got knocked up. A sweet deal all around until Casey stuck his big nose in there. It might have soured things between us, but right about then Shorty Howell up and died.

＊

I wish I could tell you that Shorty got poisoned or had his throat slashed, something exciting like that, but the truth is he just died one night like an eighty year old will. We hadn't seen him for a couple of days but didn't think anything of it until we saw an ambulance out there one morning, and out comes a body on a stretcher—Shorty—although they had his face covered.

After the ambulance left, there was this guy standing there, fiftyish, so we went over and asked him what happened to Shorty. "He died," he said. Looked like his heart gave out, probably. I figured the guy must be Shorty's son, but he said he wasn't related. Shorty didn't have any close relatives as far as he knew. Turns out the guy was the landlord. We always thought Shorty owned that house, but he just rented.

Casey and I went back into our apartment and sat down at the kitchen table across from each other, not making eye contact. We sat there quite a while. I kept waiting for Casey to say something, but I didn't have all day, I had places to go and people to meet, so I broke the ice. "Ol' Shorty would have wanted us to have that watch," I said.

"I don't know about that," Casey said, slowly shaking his head. Then he sat there way too long doing nothing but shaking his head and saying over and over, "I don't know about that."

Along about the time he was about to creep me out, he finally shook himself like he'd come to some weighty conclusion and said, "Well, I don't know about that at all, but we need money, that's for damn sure. So tonight let's go get that watch."

We waited until after midnight when we were pretty sure there wasn't anybody else up and around, and then we went over to Shorty's house. I put a blanket up against the bedroom window, and Casey hit it with a baseball bat and knocked out the glass. If you don't use a blanket or burlap bag or something against a glass when you bust it, it'll sound like a shotgun going off. We Ingrams learn stuff like that about the same time we get house-broke.

We climbed through the window, each of us with one of those little flashlights with the double-A batteries because they put out enough light to see by but not enough that folks would notice it much outside the house. Took a quick look around the living room and kitchen, but there wasn't much place to put a watch there, so it was back to the bedroom.

"I'll take the chest of drawers, and you take that pile of boxes," I told Casey because why would I waste time looking through cardboard boxes? Shorty either would have had it in his pocket when he died, or he would already have taken it off and put it wherever he put it when he wasn't carrying it, likely the chest of drawers, sure as hell not a cardboard box.

After I finished the chest of drawers, I pretended to look around in the closet while Casey was still going through the boxes. It took him a while to get his fill of that.

When he finally finished with the boxes, he straightened up like an old man with a sore back and said, "You find it?"

"Sure. I found it right off the bat. I just forgot to tell you."

"Damn it to hell."

We stood there in the dark. I suggested to Casey that we might as well see what else was worth taking, but he didn't seem much interested. He just stood there thinking. I knew nothing good would come of that, but what can you do? I let him go at it.

Finally he said, "Shorty loved that watch. It was the only thing he had that was worth anything. He would have wanted to be buried in it."

"So?"

"He would have left it in a will or something that he wanted to be buried wearing it."

"So? What are you getting at?"

"So that watch is down there at the funeral home. They're fixing to bury him in it."

You've got to be careful when you're about to claim that something somebody's just said is the stupidest thing you've ever heard in your life because there's always going to be a lot of competition for that, but what Casey had just said had to be in the running.

"You mean he died with a will pinned to his shirt or something?" I asked helpfully, but Casey didn't say anything, just stood there thinking again, which made me real uneasy. And then it came to me what he was thinking.

"You don't mean—?"

"Yeah. We gotta go to that funeral home."

There are only two funeral homes in our little bitty town, and Hunter's was for black folks, so Casey and I headed down to Shady Hills Funeral Home about two in the morning.

We've always shied away from breaking into businesses because of the security alarm stuff, but we figured we wouldn't have to worry about that with a funeral home. I mean, come on, a *funeral home*? We were right. We jimmied open the back door with a pry bar and then we were inside. I tried for about the fortieth time to talk Casey out of it, telling him the whole thing was stupid, we weren't going to find that watch, et cetera, but it was like talking to a wall. So on we went.

They had some sort of dim greenish light on in there, so we didn't even have to use our flashlights. The place looked small outside but seemed a lot bigger in. It took us several minutes to find ol' Shorty. He was under a sheet on a metal table in this hospital-like room. Casey took off the sheet. My uncle Troy, to scare me once when I'd been showing my ass a bit too much, told me what happened when they got you in a funeral home. Drained the blood out of you and sewed you up here and glued you shut, there and all. Didn't scare me a bit, though, because I was young and knew that wouldn't happen to *me*, you know? But now I looked for signs of that on Shorty. I couldn't see a thing. He just looked like a little old bony greenish slab of dead meat, which is exactly what he was. He didn't have any watch on his wrist, either.

"No watch," I said to Casey. "What did you think—that you were going to find the watch tied to his ding-dong? Hell, man, that was a *Patek Phillipe*. Somebody's got that watch in his pocket right now, and that somebody's not you. You're never going to see that watch again."

Casey made a show of looking around, getting in drawers and stuff, but I could tell his heart wasn't in it. He gave it up fast and came back to the table and stood staring down at Shorty.

"You know how he got that watch?" he said. "He *saved* for it. Saved for it for fifteen years out of his social security. Ate shit and lived like a goddamn dog to save for that. Said he wanted something nice, just one thing nice in his life that he could brag on. He never married, never had no kids."

At first I thought it had to be just the weird lights, but then I knew it wasn't— Casey really did have tears in his eyes. Then it came to me. Casey hadn't broken into the funeral home to take the watch. Oh, he wanted the watch all right, needed the money for my tuition, and he for sure would have taken the watch if he'd found it, but that wasn't the main thing. The main thing was he wanted to see Shorty one last time. I let him look his fill. I figured it was the least I could do.

After all, I'd come out of this smelling like a rose. I had the watch, of course. It'd been right there in the first drawer I'd looked in, in the chest of drawers, and I stuck it in my pocket real quick and kept on pretending to look. I just didn't figure I could trust Casey with it. Probably he would have sold it and used the money on my tuition, but he's been acting too weird lately and I couldn't chance it. This way I'll get the money from the watch, and Casey will still come up with the money for the tuition even if he has to knock over a bank or take three jobs because it's important to him that I get that college degree. It'll be the first for an Ingram for damn sure.

And I *will* get that degree, and I'll make it up to Casey at some point in the future because I'm going to be making the big bucks. I'll go into business because that's where the money is. Or maybe politics because politicians always seem to wind up with their fair share and four or five other people's, too. Yes sir, business or politics either one. I figure I'm a natural for it.

PAMPLONA

It happened in July, a brutal month in Arkansas when a man with any sense will lie low and wait until dark for just about anything he has in mind. But sense didn't have much to do with what Earl Burdette found out on George Starkey's farm. The call came in the middle of the day, not a cloud in the sky as Earl drove out to George's place. Just that sun.

Earl had seen George over at the grain elevator in Prospect earlier that morning. George said he had a joke for Earl, a good one, but damn if he could remember the punch line. Earl said it would come to him as soon as he quit thinking about it, and he figured that was what happened: George had gotten home and then remembered the punch line and was calling to tell him. Must be a hell of a joke, Earl remembered thinking before he realized George wasn't in a joking mood. You couldn't tell for sure over the phone, but it sounded like George was crying.

Earl couldn't half understand what George was saying. "Come and see what my boys done," was the only thing that came through clear.

"His boys? I go to church with George. I know for a fact him and Bessie don't have no sons," Bud Drabble, Earl's lone deputy, said when Earl told him where he was heading.

"He didn't mean sons," Earl said. "He meant his two longhorns. I'm taking the Tahoe."

Well, Deputy Dog, looks like you got what you wanted, Earl said to himself on the short drive out to George's farm because he'd been wanting some excitement on the job for a change. Not that he knew what he was going to find, but he knew it was going to be bad.

George was standing on the gravel drive that led up to his farmhouse. He looked calm enough now. "This way," he said with a jerk of his head when Earl got out of the Tahoe. As they walked past the farmhouse, Earl saw a dim figure of a woman standing inside the screen door. George's wife, Bessie. She made no move to come out, didn't respond to Earl's wave. You couldn't pay Bessie Starkey not to be friendly. Yes, this was going to be bad.

Earl followed George past the tractor shed. He knew it couldn't be far. At one time George had a good-sized farm on bottom land between two ridges, the soil better than most you found in the Ozarks, but, in his seventies now, he'd sold off most of it. He'd kept a few acres, mostly pastureland for his two longhorns, "pets," other farmers said contemptuously because they couldn't account for a man who'd feed cattle he didn't intend to butcher or breed or milk or sell.

They came to the pasture and walked a little ways into it, and then Earl stopped and did what otherwise might have been a comic double-take except there was nothing funny about this, not one thing. Then he started to run, at the same time hollering back over his shoulder to George, "Why didn't you call an ambulance? You should have called an ambulance!"

George was too old to run, but he walked steadily on, and when he caught up to Earl, standing and staring down at the body of the Oetting boy, he said, "I knew an ambulance wouldn't do him any good."

Then he started to cry again.

&

"I think it was Roy that done it," George said when he'd gotten himself under control, and Earl tried to think of a single Roy in Lafayette County. But then George added, "Leastways he's got blood on his horns," and Earl understood. He looked across the field to where the longhorns stood in the shade of the big red oak.

Still, all Earl could think to say was, "You should have called an ambulance, George," and George said, "I thought I'd better call you. He didn't need an ambulance," and Earl, staring down at the boy, loosely holding his guts, the ground muddy with his blood, said again, "But you should have called one" until George ended it by saying, "Well, Earl, you ain't called one yet, have you?"

So that was when Earl finally called Bud Drabble on his cell phone. Bud had put his name on speed dial for Earl, but Earl never could remember how to use it when the time came and generally had to make two or three attempts to punch in a number correctly because of those little buttons and his big thick fingers. This time he got it right the first time and told Bud to get an ambulance out to the Starkey place and then get out here himself, fast, although he didn't know what use Bud would be. Or anyone else, for that matter.

It'd take a while for the ambulance to get down from Marseilles, the county seat fifteen miles on up US 65. There was a story behind why the county jail and sheriff's office was in tiny Prospect rather than Marseilles, but Earl had forgotten it. Folks figured he liked the arrangement since Prospect was his home town, but it'd been awhile since it'd felt like home—or anywhere else had, either, since he and his wife LeAnn had started having problems.

While they waited for the ambulance, Earl and George walked across the field to where the longhorns stood in the shade of the red oak shoulder to shoulder, as if for warmth. The taller one, the spotted one, was trembling like you see cows in Africa do on public TV when they're getting bit all over by flies and there's nothing they can do about it. He looked guilty as hell.

"Is that Roy, the big fella?" Earl asked but then saw the blood on his horns, took a step back, and fingered the strap on his pistol.

"They're gentle animals," George said. "Gentle as kittens."

"The Oetting boy might argue the point if he was in any shape to," Earl said and instantly regretted it because of the look on George's face. But saying it made him feel bad about leaving the body all alone, so they went back to it, and in a minute Bud Drabble was there with the camera taking pictures of the body and the longhorns and asking George a lot of questions Earl hadn't thought of asking but should have. His mind didn't seem to be working right. In his ten years as county sheriff and five as deputy before that he'd seen more than one dead body—heart attacks and car wrecks and tractor rollovers—but nothing like this.

The ambulance came with the coroner along for the ride. Earl hadn't thought of the coroner, either, so give another one to Bud, who Earl had always thought was just about worth the air he breathed, but it was a close call. The coroner said the boy hadn't been dead for more than two or three hours. That threw Earl, too. Teenagers any more are hardwired for getting drunk or high and doing dumb stuff, but that's at night. In the middle of a July morning, on a Tuesday? Earl just couldn't figure it.

The coroner finished up, and then they loaded the body into the ambulance. That's when Bud found the terrycloth towel that'd been under the body. He held it up to Earl and said, "What do you make of this?"

It was a big bath towel or maybe a beach towel. Red. There was some pattern in it, a figure of some sort, and lettering just visible beneath the red.

"This son of a bitch has been dyed," Bud said. He held his right hand up and rubbed his fingertips together. "Look'ee here. The dye's coming off."

"That's blood," Earl said.

After all the others left, Earl went back to talk to George. George was sitting on his front porch steps with what looked like a 30.06 across his knees. Earl sat down beside him. He took out his Bic and spiral notebook.

"I guess I ought to take down an official statement from you, George. You know, if you could kind of give me a timeline on this thing, sort of your movements this morning, when you found the body, that sort of thing."

George looked out across the fields at nothing in particular. "I guess I just lived a couple of years too long," he said.

"Naw, don't say that. Nothing about this is your fault, George."

"I don't know. When I had the farm, that was one thing. If I would have sold it so maybe somebody else could have farmed it, maybe some young man starting up his own family, maybe if I'd done that. But selling it a piece at a time, and then that—"

He gestured east down the blacktop. You couldn't see it from where they were sitting, but Earl knew what he meant: the Git-'n-Go just over the hill with the marquee out front advertizing triple-X videos. George had sold them the land to build it on.

"You know, Bessie and me was driving up to Marseilles the other day and—how far is that, a dozen, fifteen miles?—not one single point on 65 were we ever out of sight of a gas station or a souvenir stand or something. Not one single time. What are all these people doing here? Lord knows the land's no good, rocks and all. It's not even much good for pasture. Heck, the only thing that really belongs here are the squirrels and those longhorns. They could live on these hills, poor as the land is, just fine. Say, do you know longhorns came over with Christopher Columbus? Came over from Spain."

"I didn't know that," Earl said. He couldn't think of anything else to say.

George shook his head. "It don't do no good to stay too long at the dance."

Earl suddenly remembered with a feeling like going over the first hump on a roller coaster that he needed to go notify Tyler Oetting's parents. He stood up, put the pen and notebook in his pocket, and said, "Well, I guess I got all I need for now," although he hadn't written down a word.

George nodded and smiled wistfully. "Well, I guess I know what I've got to do now."

Earl looked at the 30.06, but what was the point of saying anything? Besides, the very least Earl could do for the Oettings was tell them that that longhorn had been disposed of.

As he was turning to go, once again he saw the vague form of Bessie Starkey through the screen door. He touched the brim of his Dallas Cowboys ball cap to her, but she receded further into the shadows of the house.

He was driving slowly past the Git-'n-Go, trying to think how on earth he was going to break the news to the Oettings, when he heard the first rifle shot. Then the second.

Earl sat at the Y'All Come Inn drinking coffee, but where he'd really like to be was over at the White Oak Tavern having a serious conversation with Mr. Evan Williams. He could have gotten away with it, too, because LeAnn was up in Springfield for a few days visiting her mother. He figured, though, that after the day he'd had, if he started drinking he wouldn't stop until they had to carry him home, and that wouldn't look good for a county sheriff and an election year coming up.

Ron Metralier came in and sat down at Earl's table. Janice came over and took his order. It was after six. Ron ate supper later than most folks in Prospect. That was because he was from Little Rock and on top of it had gone off back east to law school. Catholic, too. Spoke French and Spanish and probably Latin, too, based on him being the one who'd called Earl's first decade as Lafayette County sheriff the "Pax Burdette," which hurt Earl's feelings because he thought Ron was saying "pox Burdette." Earl knew what the pox was and didn't care to have his name associated with it.

"You look like you've been rode hard and put up wet," Ron said, and Earl said, "I don't feel half that good."

"I heard about it—some of it, anyway. I don't envy you that visit you had to make to the Oettings."

Earl looked down at his coffee. "It was a day's work, all right." After he'd talked to the Oettings, he was wringing with sweat and had to go home and take a shower. Then he'd come down to the Y'All Come Inn and tried to eat a piece of Edna Conrad's coconut cream pie but couldn't get it down. He'd been drinking coffee ever since and had the shakes.

"Got any idea what happened out there?" Ron asked. Earl shook his head and then after a minute said, "Kids," but both of them knew that didn't explain anything.

"That Oetting boy was always kind of funny," Earl said.

"What do you mean? Gay?"

"No, hell no. Aw, I don't know."

Not gay, though. He always had some girl or other hanging on him. He'd gotten the basketball coach at the high school all upset when he tried to get a soccer team going and two of the basketball players signed the petition. The school board had nipped that soccer stuff in the bud, though, thank the Lord. The boy never played any other sports that Earl knew of, but he did star in the musical the junior class put on last spring—*South Pacific*—and did such a good job it made you uncomfortable to watch. Earl didn't mention any of that to Ron, though, because he sort of suspected Ron wouldn't understand. Little Rock. Catholic. Hard to figure how the two of them got to be such good friends, but there had to be something in the fact that Earl was the only friend Ron had made since he'd moved to Prospect, and Ron was the only real friend Earl had despite living there all his life. Had to be something, but Earl didn't want to think about what that something was.

"I feel sort of guilty about it myself," Earl said, holding on to that coffee cup like he was trying to warm his hands.

"I can't wait to hear this explanation."

"Yeah, I know, it's stupid, but ever since you made that Pax Burdette crack—"

"I told you I meant that as a compliment."

"I know, ten years on the job and the biggest crime wave was when the Goetz brothers were driving up and down back roads playing mailbox baseball. Hell, it must be half a dozen years since I even busted anybody for growing a marijuana crop."

"Count your blessings, Earl. I do. That's why we moved here."

"Bingo. That's just it. I should be happy, but here I was feeling sorry for myself because when I go to the state convention of county sheriffs I don't have any good stories to swap. You know what my cousin Bo Sheffield calls me?"

Ron smirked. "Barney Fife, when he's not calling you Deputy Dog."

"Laugh, sumbitch. But I think all the real sheriffing got over with about the same time they quit riding horses."

Then he remembered the Oetting boy. He'd wished for that, wished for some story to swap with the other county sheriffs. He shook his head bitterly, thinking of that poor kid and then of George Starkey saying he'd stayed too long at the dance.

"You know what George Starkey was getting ready to do when I left him this afternoon?"

Ron shook his head.

"Shoot those two longhorns of his."

Janice had brought Ron his open-faced roast-beef sandwich, Ron's favorite, but now he pushed it away.

The next morning Bud told Earl that he had run down some of Tyler Oetting's friends last night, but none of them claimed to have any knowledge of what Tyler was doing out on George Starkey's farm. Not that Bud believed a word of it, of course. It was a good bet that Tyler hadn't been out there by himself. Bud was going to go into the high school and talk to Jack Van Der Kamp, the principal, and then try to scare up some of Tyler's teachers, if any of them were in town this time of year. Maybe he'd get some insight into what made the boy tick. In the meantime Bud said that Earl ought to go back out to George's and get that statement he'd intended to get yesterday.

It was on the tip of Earl's tongue to tell Bud he needed to remember who was the Injun and who was the chief around here, but he was afraid of what reply he'd get.

He drove out to George's. He got out of the Tahoe and stood there a moment saying to himself, *Now, what's wrong with this picture?* It was a day just like yesterday, not a cloud in the sky but not too hot yet this early in the morning, a slight breeze, the two longhorns standing by the pasture gate looking at him like it was about time he showed up. And then it came to him.

"Oh, shit," he said as he turned and ran toward the house. "Oh shit oh shit oh shit oh shit."

He ran across the porch and through the unlocked screen door. "Oh, shit." George was lying in the doorway between the living room and the kitchen, the rifle balanced on his chest like someone had set it there just as careful. Bessie was on into the kitchen on her back on the linoleum. George had shot her first, of course, and then himself.

Earl ran back out to use the CB radio to call for an ambulance—even though he knew there was no reason for running or for an ambulance, either—before he remembered he didn't have a CB radio anymore. When the county had replaced the old sheriff's car with the Tahoe, they decide it'd be cheaper just to pay Earl's cell phone bill. It took Earl four tries to get the number punched in right.

When he finally got through to Bud and told him what he'd found, Bud said, "Shee-it!"

Earl spent the rest of the day dealing with the ambulance and coroner and filling out paperwork and trying to get hold of the Starkeys' son-in-law (their only child, a daughter, had died of cancer some years ago) at the same time that he tried to dodge the news crew that had come up from Little Rock and wanted to interview him. He delegated that job to Bud, who didn't seem to mind at all.

It was a long enough day that Ron Metralier beat him to the Y'All Come Inn for supper. Supper away from home two nights in a row. Things must have been frosty again between Ron and his wife.

Earl's stomach wasn't ready for a full meal, so he just ordered coffee and pie, lemon meringue this time. But his stomach wasn't ready for pie, either.

"You're going to make yourself sick over this," Ron said.

"Just explain to me what's going on, and I'll get my appetite back."

Ron pushed some peas into his mashed potatoes.

"Yesterday I was thinking that time was passing me by," Earl said, "but now I wish it would have. Problem is it hasn't passed me one shitting inch. It's dragging me right along with it, only I don't want to go where it's going."

"Problem is trying to figure where that is," Ron said.

"All I know for sure is I don't want to live in a world where stuff like this can happen and there's no answer or explanation for it."

"Well, my friend, this is the only world you get."

"Is that what they taught you in law school back East? I hope they threw in a cup of coffee and a good cigar with it because, ol' buddy, you paid too much tuition," Earl said, and Ron was about to say something back when Earl's cell phone went off.

Earl cussed at the phone for about fifteen seconds before he answered it. It was Bud. Bill Huggins, who lived on down the road from George Starkey, called in to report there was somebody fooling around the Starkey place. Some kid. Bud asked Earl if he wanted him to go and check, and Earl wanted that so bad he almost cried, but he said, no, he'd do it.

He drove back out there.

The sun was dropping down behind the ridge to the west. The pasture was half in shade and half in sun, the longhorns in the sun end, but in the shade of the red oak. Earl would have to ask Bill Huggins to look after them until some judge decided what to do with them.

Earl had seen the girl's car, a hot-pink Volkswagen bug, parked in front of the farmhouse, but he didn't see her at first glance because she was in the shade end of the pasture. She wasn't making any effort to hide. In fact, she pretty much ignored him as he let himself through the gate and crossed the pasture toward her. She was walking in big circles, peering down at the ground. She seemed to be searching for something. Earl had thought she was a boy when he first saw her because of her short blond hair. Maybe that was the new style. Hell, he didn't even know the old style.

"Hi," he said gently, like you'd speak to some skittish animal. But she didn't spook. She looked up quickly, said "Hi," and went back to her circling, searching.

He noticed she had a book, a paperback, in her hand. She must have seen him looking at it because she stopped, held the book up, and said, "I found the book, but I can't find the cape."

"Cape?"

"Tyler's cape."

"You were out here with Tyler Oetting?"

"Sure," she said brightly.

"You're . . . I don't recollect your name."

"Jen Echols."

"Oh yeah. Bob and Clare Echols' girl."

She didn't say anything to that but went back to circling.

"Can you tell me what happened out here, Jen? I mean, you know, Tyler and the steer. What were you all doing out here? Why did the steer attack him?"

She looked up with that bright smile again, just short of giggling. "We were *bullfighting*, of course," she said. She waved the book at him. "Like in here."

He went over and took the book from her. "I'll need this. You can probably get it back after we close the investigation."

"What about the cape?"

"The . . . Oh, you must mean the towel. You all dyed it red."

This time she did giggle. "Did it in the bathtub and now the bottom of the tub is all stained. I figured Mom would have a conniption, but I didn't care because we were running away to Pamplona, anyway. Do you think I'll get the cape back, too?"

"I don't think you'll want it. It's all soaked up with blood."

"Oh. Well, I could use Spray 'n Wash on it. Or do you think that would make the dye come out?"

He followed the girl back to her house and told Mrs. Echols that Jen wasn't in any legal trouble that he knew about, but they should keep an eye on her because even though she was acting fine you couldn't tell what was going on in a teenager's head. As he got back into the Tahoe, the girl waved to him from her bedroom window.

Earl passed the book across the table to Ron Metralier, who was still sitting where Earl had left him in the Y'All Come Inn. Ron lived in a big house on the edge of Prospect with his wife, Sarah, from Philadelphia, which she bowed down and prayed toward five times a day. They'd never had any children.

Ron turned the book this way and that like it was something he'd lost long ago and was delighted to have back.

"*The Sun Also Rises!*"

"It's all in there, the girl said. Why they did it. They were going to run off and fight bulls in this Pamplona place. It's in there, apparently. Pamplona."

"Yeah, it's a festival in July. Guess that's why they picked now to do it." Ron tapped the cover. "This is a great book. You ought to read it."

Earl shook his head. "*Silas Marner* freshman year in Mrs. Johnson's class did me in. I haven't had much use for novels and such since then. Why don't you do your civic duty and give me the short version."

"Well, it's a sort of love story, I'd guess you'd say."

"The hero is a bullfighter?"

"No. Well, there is a bullfighter in it, but there really is no hero as such. The central character, this American, Jake Barnes, was castrated in the war—World War I—and his lady love is a nympho."

Earl slapped the table and barked out a laugh. "Sweet Jesus, you can't make this stuff up."

Ron smiled. "Well, Hemingway did."

Earl shook his head. "So this is what Tyler Oetting and Jen Echols were patterning themselves after. This was their idea of a good time."

Ron shrugged. "It's hard to explain, but it might be attractive to young people who feel out of place, like they don't belong in the world they live in."

"There's a lot of that going around," Earl said.

Earl thought that LeAnn might be back from Springfield by the time he got home, but as he drove up he saw that the house was dark. Then, although he'd never framed the idea clearly until that moment, he knew she wasn't coming back to him, had known from the moment she said she was going to visit her mother in Springfield. Had known it long before that, probably. Their son Jeffrey was out on his own now, and there was no need for them to pretend they were making a home. What would he do with his life now? Maybe take up fishing.

He went in and turned on every light in the kitchen and den and poured himself a tall bourbon. His cell phone rang. He unhurriedly drank the bourbon but finished it before the phone stopped ringing, so he answered it.

It was Bud, of course. It was on the tip of Earl's tongue to say, *Somebody better be dead*, but he wisely held off on that one.

Bob Echols had just called him, Bud said. The girl had gone off somewhere, and they were worried about her. Earl cranked his wrist around to look at his watch because he'd never gotten in the habit of looking at the time on his cell phone. It was only a little past nine. Bud seemed to read his mind. "I told Bob it as way too early to be worried about anything, she was probably just out with her friends, but he sounded kind of shook up, which I guess is understandable considering, you know. So I told him I'd check around with the kids on the street and see if anybody knows where she is. She'll probably turn up before long."

"Probably."

Earl hung up before Bud could make any suggestions about what he should be doing. He poured himself another bourbon but then set it on the counter and stared at it a minute. He went back out and got in the Tahoe.

Jen's car was parked where it'd been earlier that day, in front of the Starkey house, like she'd come to pay a visit.

Earl got out of the Tahoe and reached under the seat and took out the big four-battery flashlight. As he walked toward the pasture, he swept the bluish light left to right and almost immediately hit the two longhorns. He'd forgotten to talk to Bill Huggins about looking after them. Their eyes gleamed with reflected light. They looked terrified.

It took him longer to find Jen, but that was because he was looking too far off into the pasture when she was standing not twenty feet from him by the pasture gate. She squinted into the light but otherwise didn't seem frightened or even surprised to see him.

As he approached her, she swung the gate open for him and said, "Did you bring the cape?"

Even now, the last days of a hot summer, the shadows are long and cool in the halls. Is anything more silent than a school building empty of children? Nothing here but my footsteps reverberating down the hall, echoing back to me. How have we come to this, September, and no children?

Last year they marched them in guarded by the 101st Airborne, bayonets fixed. I counted Nigger Go Home carved in eighty-six desks.

"What you can't sand out, we'll just have to replace," Virgil Blossom, the superintendent, said, "although I'll be damned if I know where we'll come up with the money."

Instead of getting rid of the desks, they got rid of Blossom, a good man just trying to do his job, the way I see it. Caught a tiger by the tail and couldn't let go.

Central High Tigers, class of '57. The last one, maybe, ever. What are these kids going to do now that Faubus has closed the schools?

"Hut hut, HUT!"

Except for football.

I cut into the English 120 classroom and look out the window at the Tigers in their dirty practice uniforms. I don't pretend to be a smart man. Take somebody a lot smarter than me to figure out how you can shut down school for a whole year but pass a special law so they can still have their football season. Gives us something to do, though, cleaning up the showers and locker room after each practice and sweeping out the hallways. If it wasn't for that . . .

I go back out into the main hallway and continue on down toward Claude Ireland's office. From each open doorway the afternoon sun throws a glaring shaft of light across the waxed floor. Normally we don't wax them when school's in session. The kids track in water on their shoes, and a waxed hall will get slippery as ice. I still can't forget the sound young Billy Tevis's head made when he ran in with snow on his shoes and went down on the steps. I knew he was dead before I got to him. January, 1949. Some good memories here, some bad ones.

Now they've closed it down so the white kids won't have to sit next to the coloreds. I don't know if it's right or not. Not my business to think about it. All I know is, now we can wax the floors and don't have to do anything else but sweep them once a week. Look how they shine, in bright rectangles, in between the larger areas of cool, dark shadows.

"We" wax them I say. I'm past that myself, been booted upstairs to Custodial Supervisor for the whole Little Rock School District. Stick around in any job long enough and something is bound to happen to you, good or bad. I haven't figured which this is yet.

If this integration business hadn't come up, I would have had forty to fifty men working under me, but I've had to let most of them go. Before he was given his walking papers himself, I talked Mr. Blossom into keeping one custodian per school, but the truth is, me and two or three good men could take care of most everything.

I pause outside Claude's office and put my ear to the door. Yes, I hear him in there, rocking away in that joke he nigger-rigged out of two broken desks and the seat from a worn-out swivel chair. I tap at the door.

"You in there, Claude?"

"Now where else would I be, Tom?" his voice comes back deep and liquid, like it was rising out of a slow, muddy river.

I go on in. There he sits in his "office"—the maintenance room, of course—surrounded by his mops and brooms and pails of wax, varnish, and various cleaners.

Claude must be about my age I'd guess from the grey hair that circles in a band around his head, although it's hard to tell with a colored man. I'm always intending to check his age in his employment records, but I keep forgetting.

We go back a long ways, Claude and me. I wouldn't be surprised if he hasn't been working for the district longer than I have. He'd been here at Central for a number of years by the time I transferred over from Pulaski Heights Junior. He's a good man. Knows his job, shows up for work on time, doesn't complain, a fellow you can talk to. That's why when I had to pick one of the four custodians at Central to keep on, I chose Claude. Not a popular decision in some quarters, let me tell you. Didn't know when I took this job I'd have to be a politician, too, but sometimes it works out that way.

"So, Claude. What do you know for sure?"

He shrugs, lifts his hands, fingertips and palms pink.

"Mile's a long row to hoe. That's about it."

"Keeping busy?"

"Oh, sure. Mowing the grounds and pruning take about one morning a week, then I probably spend about a good half hour cleaning out the showers and locker room after morning and afternoon practice. That only leaves me about six, seven hours a day on the average to sit here and rock."

"Nice work if you can get it," I nod and smile, but Claude looks away, and something close to a grimace pinches his otherwise glossy, wrinkleless face.

"Guess so, for a man like to sit on his behind all day."

Claude's a good man, but hard to figure sometimes, hard to read his moods. Like when I told him at the beginning of the summer that I was letting everybody else go but keeping him on. I didn't expect him to get down and kiss my big toe or anything. But still, it was a hard decision, and I took some heat for it. Chick Penney threw a conniption fit. "Let me go and keep that nigger, keep that nigger?" Getting right in my face, his fists clenched, a man half my age. No, Claude didn't have to kiss my foot or even say thank you, but *something*, just some sign that he knew what it took, what it cost me, keeping him on. But not a thing from him, just nodded like that was what he'd expected all along and asked, "So, you want me to go ahead and strip the gym floor, or put that off for a while?"

Hard to read.

I look around the supply room, notice a desk with a pad sander on top of it. Almost forgot I told him at the beginning of the summer to try to get that Nigger Go Home stuff out of as many of those desks as he could.

I nod toward the desk: "How you coming with the sanding?"

He cuts a glance toward the desk, looks away.

"Oh, I do about one ever two or three days. Don't want to do too many—cut into my rockin' chair time."

Again that note of almost bitterness in his voice.

"Are you able to get it out?"

"Probably 'bout one out of three. Them boys cut too deep on most of them. Sand down far enough to get it all off, won't have no desk top."

I shake my head sadly but can't think of anything else to add.

"Well," I finally say, "guess I'd better head over to Horace Mann and see how Robinson's doing."

Claude nods: "Say hi at him for me."

"That I'll do."

I walk out of the supply room, close the door after me, turn to go back down the hall. Through the open door of the home ec room, the afternoon sun slants down out of the tall, shadeless windows, almost blinding me. But then another two steps and I'm back in the dark again.

Late fall, almost winter by the calendar, but you couldn't tell it, me in my shirtsleeves.

In the hallways of Central High, the shadows are long and dark and deep.

I pause outside Claude's office door, tap twice.

"It ain't locked."

Claude's sitting in his makeshift rocker, but he's not rocking. He looks slightly dazed. Has he been sleeping?

"Hey, Claude. What do you know for sure?"

His hands tighten on the arms of the rocker.

"Hell, Tom, I don't know nothin'."

His hands relax, then tighten again, relax, then tighten.

"Claude, is there something wrong?" I ask, although I can guess.

His big white eyes roll over his high, black cheekbones. Could laugh if I thought about it—some colored boy in a movie, frightened by a "haint." Or was it TV: *Amos and Andy*?

"Chemistry room, third floor," he says, lifting his chin as if pointing the way with his broad, flat nose. "Water stain in the corner of the ceiling, 'bout the size of a barrel top. No pipes up there—must be a leak in the roof someplace."

"Damn. We just tarred that roof two summers ago."

Things have been going wrong in the school buildings. Janitors and maintenance men are more familiar than most with the natural processes of decay—mildew, mold, corrosion, rust—but we thought that with the children gone, these processes would slow down. Instead, they seem to have sped up. Worse, we thought we'd get some relief from the problems related to human use, but for no apparent reason things are breaking, falling apart, failing to function. Just yesterday the main sewer line backed up at Ish Elementary, even though no more than two or three people a day have been using the facilities there the last six months. Last week a doorknob to the art room came off in my hand at Carver, and a twelve-foot blackboard fell off the wall at McDermott. It's something different every day. Even at Hall, the new school, I had to move Bud Alexander over from Bale afternoons to help out John Cosco with all that's been going wrong.

Central has been no harder hit than the others, but Claude has taken it bad. Something is happening that he can't understand, I guess, and he almost seems frightened by it. Not two weeks ago, on Thanksgiving Day, he called me up at home to tell me a basketball goal had broken loose in the gym and was hanging by one bolt. I almost lost my temper then, but there was something in his voice . . . And what on earth was he doing there Thanksgiving Day?

I tried to talk to him, told him it was just like a house when all the people moved out. Ever see how fast an empty house goes to pot?

"That's it!" he said, eyes gleaming. "It ain't natural. A house should have a family in it, and school should have children. It's wrong, Tom, wrong."

"Well, we can't do anything about it," I said, "just fix it when something breaks."

For a while I thought my talk helped him, but I finally figured out he just traded one over-reaction for another. Instead of spending all hours at the school, calling me up on holidays and weekends and late at night, trying to fix things before they broke, he now mostly sits and broods, acts like he's afraid to set foot outside his office. I about have to take a whip to him to get him to do anything.

"Well, Claude," I say, "you been up there to check it out yet?"

The roof I meant. But I know the answer.

He shakes his head slowly, that sad, dazed look on his face.

"No, I ain't been up there yet."

"Well, don't you think you ought to?"

"Reckon I had," he says.

But he doesn't move from the chair.

February.

The dust is so thick on the hallways that I could imagine snow has somehow drifted in under the doors and covered everything with a pale blanket. Except that we have had no snow this winter. Instead, we have clouds and drizzle and a raw wet wind, and I shiver as I walk through the cold, dark, silent shadows of Central High.

The toes of my shoes scuff up dust as I walk, and as I trail my fingertips along the walls they come away bearded with dust. It must have been three weeks, a month, since Claude has so much as run a broom down these hallways.

I pause before the school counselor's office. Yes, still there: the broken glass in the door, crack running from lower left corner to upper right. Time after time after time I've told him to fix it.

I feel my hackles rising as I march off toward Claude's office. I give the supply room door two quick raps with my knuckles but open it without waiting for a reply.

And there he sits, as he's been sitting day after day after day for . . . how long now? Instead of shutting down the furnaces completely, we keep the thermostats in all the buildings set at fifty to hold down dampness that could damage the walls, ceiling tiles, floor joints—everything—but, still, it's cold enough that Claude wears his old navy pea coat and gloves. The way he rolls his head over and looks at me with those watery-yellow eyes—I used to think they're white, but I've since looked closer—he looks like an invalid, or someone trying to recover from a high fever.

Every time I come to Central I see how Claude has just let things slide, and I get angry. I charge into his office ready to tell him what I think—that he's let me down, that I'm sorry I kept him on and let others go. I come in ready to tell him he's through at Central High. But then I see him sitting there looking the way he looks, and I can't bring myself to say any of the things I'd planned on.

But why not? What's holding me back? I don't understand myself any better than I understand Claude.

I try to smile.

"Well, Claude, what do you know for sure," I say.

But he stares at me and says nothing.

Spring has come. The redbuds, dogwoods, and jonquils have been glorious, and now the azaleas are blooming. Claude has planted a row of them under the windows of the administrative offices at the front of the building, and already the buds have begun to open: a red bush, a pink, and a white, red, pink, and white under the sparkling clean windows. Yes. in addition to planting azaleas and trimming all the hedges, Claude has washed the windows, swept out the halls, and shampooed the carpet in the principal's office, for, with the spring, Claude Ireland seems to have come back to life.

I wish I could say I was happy, but something is still not right at Central High. Standing in the cool, dark shadows of the hallways, I have heard voices, I could swear it. I began to hear them about the same time Claude went back to cleaning and fixing, began to smile and joke almost like his old self. But I can't connect these two things—the voices and Claude's return to life—and I can't locate the voices. Sometimes it seems like they grow louder when I move into the north end of the building, louder still when I go up to the third floor. But always at some point I stop hearing them altogether. And then I wonder: did I just imagine it?

"Must be hearing them ol' Central High ghosts," he'll joke when I mention it.

But he'll go out with me to explore, hollering out as we move through the hallways, "Stay where you be, ghosts! Don't go jumping out and scaring the daylights out of us!" Then he'll laugh.

Often lately Claude's met me at the back entrance, which must mean sometimes he watches for my car to pull into the parking lot behind the school. That's the reason why today I've parked on the side street and entered the building through the front, unlocking and swinging open the big door as quietly as possible. It's just past seven, at least an hour earlier than I've come since school was last in session.

The halls are silent. I hear nothing. Nothing at all, and yet *something* is there, isn't it?—not a sound but a sort of ripeness, a readiness for sound, as if it's coming or is already there, just around the corner.

I turn to my right and walk toward the stairs at the north end of the building. Before I reach them I hear it: voices, laughter perhaps. Then nothing. I strain to hear, but . . . nothing. Again the feeling that perhaps I've imagined it.

I begin to climb the stairs, and before I'm to the second floor I hear the sounds again, unmistakable now, not imagining: voices.

I run up the stairs—or at least come as close to running as this sixty-year-old can manage—catch my toe on a step, almost go down. The voices stop.

I walk on up to the third floor, not bothering to be quiet now, no point to it. I listen but hear nothing. Everything seems normal, but something is wrong. Then I notice it. One of the classroom doors is closed. Mathematics 303. I walk over to the door, test the knob. Not locked. I open the door.

Old habits are hard to break. The custodian of thirty years in me wonders what Claude did with all the desks even before I wonder who the people are. The man and woman standing by the windows, the little boy, almost a baby, on the floor with a pull toy, the two girls—twins maybe—sitting on a folding bed, one holding a piece of bread covered with jam or jelly. Pushed up end-first against the wall opposite the folding bed are three cots.

All five of them look at me, white eyes staring out of black faces.

I close the door and head back down the stairs.

I meet Claude between the first and second floors coming up the stairs.

"My niece and her family. From McGehee," he says before I can say anything. "Up here looking for work."

"You know they can't stay here, Claude."

"Only gonna be until Joe gets a job and finds 'em a place."

"No. They can't stay here."

"Why not, Tom?"

"You know why, Claude. It's not right."

"Oh, I see, not right. It's right for them to kill this school, though, that it? Making them children stay home's like cutting the heart out of this school, gutting it like you'd gut a catfish."

"That doesn't have anything to do with this, and you know it, Claude."

"Oh, I know that, do I?"

We stare at each other. "I'll give you until the day after tomorrow to get them out of here, Claude. That's it."

We stare at each other. Claude is half-a-head taller than me, so I edge up a step. Now we stare at each other, eye to eye.

꧁

I give him a week.

For one week I don't return to Central. I spend most of my time at Hall High, a brand new school that after almost a year of no classes still smells of wet plaster, fresh paint, sawdust. Not a student set foot in it and already the furnace is out and we can't figure out what's wrong with it. Claude's right—don't use a thing for what it's meant for, and it begins to die. Still, to let that family in there . . . some things can be done and some just can't.

Monday morning. I've given him a full week, but I don't have much hope of things turning out well. A bad business from the start.

I enter Central my old way, through the rear doors. Claude's not there waiting for me, watching. I head right up to the third floor.

I smell them—their presence—even before I hear them. Bacon frying. The door's not closed. I don't go in, just stand there looking through the open door: the husband with his feet propped up on the radiator, reading a newspaper, wife combing her hair into a mirror hanging by a string from the corner of the blackboard, children here and there. None of them bother to look at me.

Then I smell the bacon frying again. Not here. I follow my nose down the hall to the next classroom, Mathematics 305, and find an old man poking with a fork at bacon sizzling in a small iron skillet on a hot plate. He nods and smiles: "How do." An old woman sits at the one desk left in the room, so small her feet don't touch the floor. She waves a tiny black hand at me. I nod.

I go down to Claude's office and open the door. He's sitting in his rocker, rocking away. "Howdy, Tom. What do you know for sure?" he says brightly. But he does not smile.

"I wish I could say I knew *you*, Claude. I just don't understand you anymore."

"Oh. You must've been upstairs already. Meet my aunt and uncle? They from over around McGehee, too. Landlord raised the rent on them to where they couldn't hardly eat, so I brought 'em up here. I'm fixing up the attic at my place for 'em, so they'll only be here a little while."

"No, Claude, they're not going to be here a little while. You're going to move them out."

"Why? It ain't like they're moving in permanent. Soon as Joe finds himself a job and I get that attic fixed up . . . and hell, if they was to let the kids come back, I'd have them out in a second, you know that."

"They've got to go."

"But *why*?"

"We already talked about this."

"No we ain't. All you say is, 'They got to go, they got to go.' We ain't *talked* at all. Just give me one good reason."

"Well, it's against the law for one thing."

"The law, shit."

He puckers up like he's going to spit, but doesn't. We stare at each other, both of us breathing hard, anger tough on men our age.

"Why are you doing this to me, Claude?"

"Doing to *you*?"

"Yes, me. After what I've done for you . . ."

"What have you done for me, Tom?"

That just goes all over me. I try to keep the rage from shaking my voice.

"Didn't I let *you* keep your job when I had to let Chick Penney and the others go?"

"Chick Penney? Why in hell shouldn't you have kept me instead of Chick Penney? He'd only been here four years. I been here going on thirty. Why should you have even thought about keeping Chick Penney instead of me? . . . Oh."

I can see it dawning on him, and he looks away and laughs a short, dry bark of laugh.

I feel my anger go. Instead of angry, I just feel bad, but I don't know why. What could I do different?

"I'm coming back tomorrow, Claude, and if they're not all gone, I'm going to have to call the police. You just haven't given me any choice in this thing."

He doesn't look at me.

I turn to leave, and it's only then that I become aware of all the desks around me, piled one on top of another, almost filling the room.

"What are these?" I ask, turning around in a complete circle.

"Ones I couldn't get 'nigger' off of," Claude says.

"Oh. Well, get rid of these, too."

"Yessir," Claude says matter-of-factly, like nothing has ever happened between us.

Tuesday morning, already warm, although it's not yet eight o'clock. Summer in the air.

I park on the side street and enter Central through the front door, although I'm not sure why. I'm not trying to catch anybody by surprise—no point to that. Besides, I expect them all to be gone. As I walk up to the third floor, I hear nothing, smell nothing, and I sense that no one is in the building. Sure enough, Mathematics 303 and 305 are empty. The cots and rollaways are gone, the desks have been put back, and the floors are spotless.

I go down to Claude's office. The door is open. I snap on the light. The desks have all been removed, but other than that, all seems normal. Still, something is different about the room. What, though? I snap off the light and step back into the hall. Something here, too, bothers me.

I wander down the hall, trying to put my finger on it. What is it? I don't hear anything, don't smell anything. Yes, I do! Smoke—not strong, but unmistakable now that I realize it, yes, clearly smoke in the air. I hurry down the hall, looking into classroom after classroom, rush up to the third floor, back down to the second. It's on the second floor that I by chance glance out of the window of History 232 and see the column of smoke lifting into the air behind the building.

I go out the back to the parking lot. Claude has lit the fire on the open area by the dumpsters. He often burns dead leaves and small quantities of trash there, but this blaze is huge, the flames leaping fifteen, twenty feet in the air. Claude must have set it just minutes ago, for I can still see the desks clearly, the fire wrapped around them, some near the bottom not fully caught yet. But Claude's nowhere to be seen.

At the outer edge of the bonfire, turning to char before my eyes, I spot Claude's rocker. So that was what was different about his office.

I stare at the fire until my eyes water and the flesh on my face and arms stings from the heat, then I turn away.

I don't think I'll ever see Claude again.

I must have stared at the fire too long. Spots jump when I blink and ghosts of flame dance before me as I walk back toward the school.

I open the door, stand there. I shake my head to try to clear my vision. Yes, yes, I have stared too long at the fire. The hallway before me is so black I'm afraid to move in.

Black as . . . black as . . . But I don't say it.

I knew a guy who claimed to own twenty-two square yards of land. He'd look you in the eye and say, "I own twenty-two square yards of land," just like that. It was hard to tell if he was saying it with pride or sorrow. That may be because he was an Indian. From my experience, Indians are hard folks to pin down.

He'd give his name as Norman Cuts, but after I got to know him a little better, I found out his full name was Norman Dull Knife Cuts.

"What's that mean? 'Dull Knife Cuts.' Where'd that come from?" I asked him.

"Well, I heard a lot of stories about that," he said, "all of 'em lies."

He said he was a full-blooded Oglala Sioux and had grown up on the Pine Ridge Reservation in South Dakota, but we were in Arkansas when I first met him twenty years ago. He was probably about thirty at the time, which I thought of as middle-aged. Shows you how young I was.

Those were my salad days, I guess. I was a couple of years out of high school, no family to tell me how to live my life. I was making enough money I was never out of beer but not so much I'd worry about telling the boss to go to hell. I was driving a '68 Camaro with a custom paint job, Survival Orange, real sweet. And I was living with a woman who was a bitch, but the sex was abundant. Doesn't get much better than that, hey?

The only fly in the ointment was my job—not the pay, which was fine, but the work itself. I'd hired on with McCandless Construction building a new bridge across Cheval Creek about a dozen miles outside of Little Rock. It was a wet spring, and the unpaved road down to the work site at the bottom of the gorge was a mess of slimy yellow-green clay. One day the foreman sent me on an errand to the boss's shack at the top of the hill, and I'd fallen down a hundred or two times when a pickup stopped beside me.

"You're working at it way too hard, man," the guy inside said.

It was Norman Cuts. I didn't know his name at that point, but I knew he was an Indian. I thought he was laying some of that bullshit Indian mysticism on me with that "working way too hard" line.

"You mean if I take it slower I'll get there faster?" I said.

"No, I mean you get in the pickup and you'll get there faster," he said.

So I got in the pickup.

Norman was primarily a gofer, running back and forth to Little Rock or other McCandless work sites. I said that sounded like a good job. About one more day on the shovel, I said, and I was either going to quit or wedge the shovel up that fat foreman's ass. Norman said he could understand that, and by the time we made it to the top of the hill we were good friends.

"Hey, maybe I could get you working with me. I need some help goferin'," he said as we sat in the pickup drinking coffee from his thermos, me using the thermos cap and Norman a Styrofoam cup he fished out from under the front seat. Even though it was spring, a light mist was falling, and it was chilly enough you could see your breath. Inside the cab, though, the heater working fine, the coffee good and hot, it felt great.

"I could go for that," I said. "But the foreman hates my guts. How you going to talk him into it?"

"Oh, that's easy. Eldon Holt is afraid of me. He thinks I'm a crazy Indian and I'll cut his gizzard out if he looks cross-eyed at me."

"What gives him that idea?"

"Maybe this," he said and pulled from somewhere inside his shirt a Bowie knife about a foot long by five pounds of stainless steel.

"Shee-it! You ever cut anybody with that?"

"Yeah, me."

He held up his left hand. An ugly white scar ran from the middle of his palm across his thumb-pad to his wrist.

"Tried to open a beer can I'd broken the tab off of. Take some advice from a crazy Indian: use a can-opener for that."

From then on I worked with Norman in the pickup. One day he invited me over to his place after work. He was kind of down—broke up with his woman or something—and I think he needed some company. He lived in a trailer in Ferndale, just west of Little Rock. We drank a lot of beer. That's when he told me his full name, Norman Dull Knife Cuts, which he almost never used because it took too long to write if you were writing it yourself and too long to explain if you were giving the name to someone else.

"Besides," he said, "if you have to explain it, they'll never understand it anyway."

That sounded like one of those wise old Indian things, which was crap, because it didn't take me long to figure out that Norman was damn near as clueless as I was. But like I said, we'd drunk a lot of beer, and I liked his slow way of saying things like he'd been thinking about them a long time.

That was also the first time he told me about his twenty-two square yards of land.

"You mean acres?"

"No, yards. Wanna go see it?"

"Sure. Whereabouts is it?"

"On the Pine Ridge Reservation, in South Dakota."

That was the first time I'd heard of Pine Ridge, but I'd heard of South Dakota. It was a long way from Arkansas, which suited me just fine. I was feeling tied down in Little Rock, anyway. McCandless Construction will work you half to death and give you shit on top of it, and the bitch I was living with was starting to get on my nerves, nagging me all the time about getting married and crap like that. So I was ready to put a few hundred miles between me and Little Rock.

"I'm ready to go," I said.

"I could tell you would be."

Well, I wasn't quite ready. If I bailed out on my half of the apartment lease, it'd be just like that bitch to change the locks, and I'd play hell getting my stuff back. So I told Norman I wanted to go by my apartment first to get some things.

"Okay. I ain't in no hurry."

By then it was about two in the morning, which I figured was great because Phyllis—that was the bitch's name—worked the night shift at Baptist Medical Center. Just my luck, though, I walked in and there she was waiting for me. She looked like she'd been crying.

"What the hell are you doing here?" I said.

"I told you before you went to work this morning that I had the day off. We were supposed to eat buffet at Pizza Hut tonight. I told you."

I didn't know what to say to that, so I didn't say anything. I went into the bedroom and started cramming clothes into an AWOL bag. Phyllis stood in the door watching me.

"Where are you going?" she said. Her voice was trembling.

"Pine Ridge," I said.

"Pine Ridge? Where's that?"

"West of here. McCandless is sending me over there on a job for a couple of weeks. They've got a trailer over there they let you stay in, no charge."

I got nervous with her standing there watching me, so I took what I had and walked past her into the living room. I turned, and we stood there looking at each other a minute. I was hoping she'd go back into the bedroom or the bathroom or something so I could unhook the stereo. The speakers weren't anything to brag about, but the receiver was a Pioneer, and I didn't want to leave it behind. But she didn't look like she was going anywhere, so I said, "Well, I'll see you later."

"Bull*shit* you will!" she said. Not said but hollered. Like hollering was going to make any difference.

We were an hour outside of Little Rock before I realized that we were in a McCandless Construction pickup. When I pointed this out to Norman, he nodded and said, "Yeah, runs real good. My Plymouth needs a new alternator, and I didn't think it was a good idea to set out on a long trip in it."

It took two or three days to get to Pine Ridge. Norman did all the driving. We'd drink beer for a while, and then he'd pull over and we'd sleep for a few hours, and then we'd set off again. Hell of a time.

It was late in the afternoon when we finally got to the Pine Ridge Reservation. I don't know what I expected, teepees or something, I guess, but there wasn't anything like that. A little town and a lot of Indians.

"I've never seen so many Indians in my life," I said.

"Neither have I," Norman said. He said it like it was a wonderful thing, but I didn't see much wonderful about Pine Ridge. It looked about as sorry as some of the little towns I'd been through in Arkansas.

We didn't spend much time in the town but drove straight on through. A couple of miles on the other side we turned off the main road onto this little road that was more like a path. I didn't think there would be anybody living down a road like that, but there were little houses and house trailers left and right for miles, it seemed like, yards full of rusted-out trash barrels and old tires and beer bottles and so many burned-out cars it looked like a war zone. We kept winding around until the houses finally started to thin out, and I began to get a little worried.

"You're going to get our asses lost," I said.

For some reason this seemed to get Norman borderline pissed. "Your ass couldn't get any more lost than it already is," he said.

I didn't want to be out in the middle of nowhere with a drunken Indian carrying a Bowie knife, so I shut up.

A minute or two after that he pulled off to the side of the road and stopped. I thought he was going to kick me out or stick that Bowie knife between my ribs, but instead he nodded out the window and said, "There it is."

"There what is?"

"My twenty-two square yards of land."

I looked, but all I could see was the same dusty ground, bare of anything but weeds, a few more old tires, a few less beer bottles than in the other places we'd passed, but no house at all.

"Where exactly is it?"

"Where exactly," he repeated, not too sure himself, it seemed to me.

He got out of the pickup and wandered off into the weeds. I followed. After about twenty paces he stopped and looked around, then turned and walked a few steps the other way. He looked around some more, then looked up at me and nodded.

"Right here," he said.

He held his hands shoulder-width apart and swung them up and down and repeated, "Right here," as he took two steps and stopped. Then he turned ninety degrees to his left, swung his hands up and down again and said, "And right here," as he stepped off eleven paces.

"Two by eleven. Twenty-two square yards. My grandfather had quite a bit of land back in the '30's, but he started trading it off and selling it off a little at a time until there wasn't much left. Indians don't have much of a feel for property rights. Didn't used to, anyway. By the time it came down to my father, there were 242 square yards that the Dull Knife Cuts family still owned. He had eleven sons when he died and each got twenty-two square yards. He also had two daughters—my sisters—and he left them the cash. I think about a thousand each they wound up with. He said men needed land, but women knew better how to use money. I don't know. Sometimes I think my sisters got the best of the deal . . ."

We both looked around at the weeds, the tires, the beer bottles.

". . . and sometimes not."

I knew what I thought. I thought I'd got myself hooked up with one crazy Injun. Did he really expect me to buy all this? I didn't say anything, of course, but maybe Norman guessed what I was thinking because we didn't talk much on the way back to Little Rock, where he got arrested for stealing the pickup, and I got back into my apartment one night when Phyllis wasn't there and got my stereo. I left her with a bunch of other stuff that rightfully belonged to me, but that was okay. Back then, I traveled light.

I think I heard that Norman didn't do any time for stealing the pickup, but I wouldn't swear to it. I remember Norman real well but not too much else from back then. In fact, I'm not real clear on a lot of what has gone on over the twenty years between when I first met Norman and when I ran into him again a couple of weeks ago in Monette, Missouri. Things kind of run together. I know I've been married three times, maybe four. I've never been sure whether that one in the middle of the night in Reno was the real deal or not. But if it was, then four. (I was carrying on one of these deep philosophical conversations with this guy sitting next to me in a bar, like you will after a number of beers, when he said, "Bet you a beer you can't tell me the color of your first wife's eyes. Be honest, now." I thought and thought but by God couldn't remember what color they were. "Hey, how'd you do that?" I said. "It wasn't that hard, pal," he said, but he never did tell me what the trick was.)

For the last year or so I've been living in Springfield and working for Tibbets Brothers, one of the biggest auction houses around. Sam Tibbets runs the house itself, but I work mostly with his little brother, Sonny, traveling around doing real estate auctions at dead folks' houses. The job's not bad. You're not tied down to a certain place or schedule. You work real hard sometimes, but there's a lot of goof-off time, too. Sonny himself is an okay guy for a boss. He got religion a few years ago, but it didn't all the way take. He'll hold his cowboy hat over his heart and pray with the family of the deceased, but then every couple of weeks he'll bring in a keg of beer and get lit and tell stories about being a door-to-door lingerie salesman, getting poontang out the wazoo. Now there would be a great job.

Anyway, we were working an estate sale in Monette. Tibbets Brothers does things up right. They advertise in the paper and on the radio even for a really big sale, and they always have a refreshment stand (a camper pulled by a pickup) there selling hot dogs, hamburgers, pop, snow cones, etc. Old June Spooner had been in charge of the stand for years—drove it, did the cooking, worked the window—but she was knocked out of action by an operation for varicose veins. We did two sales with no refreshment stand at all, and then in Monette we see the stand coming up the street toward where we were setting up for the sale.

"Oh, I forgot to tell you," Sonny said. "I got somebody to take June's place. An Indian."

Now, the Springfield area is crawling with Indians, lots more than Little Rock, but for some reason, the second Sonny said that I had the strongest feeling that Norman Cuts was going to be driving that pickup. He was.

"So. Mr. Dull Knife Cuts. Still driving pickups, I see," I said, walking up to the driver's window.

He nodded. "Hi, Bobby," he said, like we'd had breakfast together that morning or something.

Right then we got ambushed by Sonny Tibbets.

"Elser, I'm not paying you to visit. Get your ass back to the house and start hauling furniture." (Sonny could be a nice guy, but only after the work was done.) "Cuts, back that camper up the drive here and set up right about there. We'll have the auction out on the front lawn."

"Okay, boss," Norman said.

It's a lot of work setting up for an auction. Hauling the large items—furniture, large appliances, etc.—is the easy part. It's the small stuff that takes time. We set up long tables—plywood sheets across saw horses—and lay out everything that can possibly sell: glasses, dishes, pots and pans, knickknacks, picture frames, books, pens and pencils, towels, bedding, radios, ball gloves, cans of paint thinner and kerosene, canning jars, old tools, damn near anything but foodstuffs and generally clothes, although sometimes clothes, too.

Sonny works on a tight schedule, and you normally have to hump it until the auction itself starts, but then you can relax a little, unless you have to help some little old lady carry something to her car. I like to watch Sonny call the auction. He puts on quite a show, cracking jokes, trading good-natured insults, sometimes singing a country song—getting the folks in a friendly mood so they'll part with a little more of their money.

I'd almost forgotten about Norman, but—wouldn't you know it?—before Sonny got halfway through the small items a light rain started to fall, so I sought shelter under the awning over the refreshment stand service window and chatted with Norman as Sonny went on with the sale.

"Look at that woman. She's crying," Norman said.

"What woman?"

"Over there."

Then I saw who he was talking about, a woman about Norman's age standing with a man and two other women, right out in the open, not under a tree or anything. They were the family that the sale was being held for. It was their mother or father or something that had died.

"It's just the rain on her face, Norman."

"It ain't right, letting all their stuff sit out in the rain like this. What they accumulated over their whole lives, and now it's just sitting out in the rain."

"Come on, Norman, don't get all bent out of shape. It's not their stuff, anyway. It was their mother's or father's or whoever the hell it was."

"Yeah, but they probably grew up with it. It's probably their heritage, man."

"Well, what do you expect Sonny to do? Have us haul it all back into the house? It took over an hour to get it all out here."

"I guess, but those folks ain't happy about it. Look at her—crying. And why's the boss still on the chickenshit stuff? Listen to him. He's trying to get 'em up to a buck on salt and pepper shakers, and there's the sofa and bed and refrigerator and stuff sitting there getting wet."

"You gotta sell the small stuff first, Norman, or else nobody would stick around for it after the big stuff's gone. Besides, maybe that's what the woman is crying about. Little things like that have a lot of sentimental value to some people."

"You got a point there, Bobby."

The rain let up some, and I walked over to Sonny's Suburban to see if there was a keg of beer in the back. No such luck. When I got back to the refreshment stand, Norman was gone. What the hell?

Then I spotted him at the rear of the circle of people surrounding Sonny. He had the salt and pepper shakers cradled in his left hand with his right hand raised like he wanted to answer a question for the teacher.

"Two dollars," he called out.

Sonny gave him a long, murderous look and then said, "Sold to the Indian for two dollars."

Faye Reynolds, who handled the money-end of the auction, took two dollars from Norman and stuck it in her cigar box and then handed him this ceramic thing, a horse or something. Next, Norman bought this raggedy doll thing that looked like it was homemade, then a vase with a dead flower in it, then a shoe box full of costume jewelry that Sonny started at thirty dollars and Norman bought for three.

When he'd bought all he could hold in his arms, Norman made his way back to the stand and lined the stuff up on the counter next to the snow-cone machine.

"What're you going to do with all that stuff, Norman?"

He just shrugged, but he had a little smile on his face like he was mighty pleased with himself. I could have told him, any time you start getting pleased with yourself you better protect your nuts because somebody's going to come along real soon and stomp them for you.

It took an hour to finish up the sale, and then Sonny and Faye huddled in his Suburban with a pocket calculator and stacks of receipts, checks, and cash. I was helping clean up the trash and unsold stuff, and Norman was shutting down the refreshment stand. Norman finished first. Then I saw him heading across the lawn to where the man and three women—the family—were standing. He had all the stuff he'd bought cradled in his arms.

I started over in that direction. Out of the corner of my eye I noticed Sonny, coming up fast, heading toward Norman, too. By the time we got there, the family were holding the various items Norman had brought them. The three women were all crying, and the man looked like he was ready to.

Sonny stepped in front of Norman and sort of rocked from left to right on the balls of his feet and clenched his fists like it was all he could do to keep from jumping on Norman and whaling the tar out of him.

Instead, he turned to the family and said, just as sweet as you please, "Why don't you all come on over to the Suburban, and we'll see how much money we made for you?"

They moved off in that direction, but Sonny stayed where he was. He stared at Norman flat as a copperhead.

"What in the living hell do you think you're doing?"

"What do you mean, boss? What's the problem?"

Sonny turned to me like he couldn't bear to even look at Norman.

"Tell him," he said.

I did: "Look, Norman, those people don't want the stuff back. They want to get rid of it. That's why they're having the sale. It's not to make money, not primarily, anyway. It's to get rid of all that stuff."

"But some of it has sentimental value, Bobby. You said so yourself."

"That's the stuff they want to get rid of most."

Norman looked at me like, hell, that ain't right, but Sonny didn't give him time to figure it out.

"Look, Cuts, I'll pay you for today, but then I want your ass out of here. I can't afford to have a dumb Indian getting customers all upset."

Norman reached inside his shirt, and I figured, this is it, he's going to haul out that Bowie knife and gut Sonny like a largemouth bass. But instead he just scratched his side real slow like he was thinking about something that happened a long time ago. Something sad.

"That's okay, boss," he said. "This ain't no kind of job for me."

He started walking off down the street. Where was he going? It was getting dark, the rain had picked up again, and we were thirty miles from Springfield.

"Wait up, Norman. I'll give you a ride," I said.

"Where the hell you think you're going, Elser? We still got work to do here," Sonny hollered after me.

I just kept on walking.

On the way back to Springfield, Norman said he felt bad I quit my job over him. I shouldn't have done it, he said.

"Hell, that job don't mean nothing to me," I said. And I meant it. I'd made up my mind earlier that afternoon when Sonny made that crack about me getting my ass back to hauling furniture that I was going to tell him where he could stick his job.

"But it should mean something to you, man. That was a good job. I wish like hell I still had mine, man."

"What's the big deal?"

He told me. It was a woman—wouldn't you know it? Some woman in Liberal, Kansas. He'd been married to her, but they were divorced now. She threw him out because of his drinking.

"It was all my fault. I wish I was still married to her. She's a good old gal. She's got three kids. They're not my kids, but I wish they were. If I still had that job, I could send her some money."

"If they're not your kids, she can't make you pay child support. I been married three or four times, and I've never paid a damn penny in alimony."

"I wish they were my kids," was all he said.

Norman seemed to get sadder and sadder the closer we got to Springfield.

I was just about to ask him directions to his place when he said, "Hell, man, hell. When I get the blues like this, there's only one thing that helps."

"What's that?"

"Seeing my land."

"Your land?"

I should have known, I guess, but all that stuff—the first time—was a long time ago.

"You know, my twenty-two square yards."

"Oh, that's right. Up in South Dakota."

"Yep. My land."

What else did I have to do?

"Okay," I said. "Let's go."

I started out driving because we were in my car, but as soon as I figured out Norman wasn't bullshitting me when he said he'd given up drinking, I let him drive while I attacked a case of Pabst. I probably didn't drink more than half of it, though. Not that much fun drinking alone.

I couldn't tell that the reservation had changed much in twenty years. Not that I remembered a whole lot about it—beer cans, old tires, etc.—but what I remembered was still there in spades.

Norman barreled straight on through the town. A few miles the other side, he turned off onto a rutted dirt road. The same one as last time? Who could tell? There were little roads branching off from the main road every few hundred yards, and they all looked alike.

We drove until we seemed to have left behind most of the little cabins and house trailers. Then Norman pulled off to the side and parked. He looked past me out the window and sighed.

"Well, here we are. There's my land."

What the hell was I doing there? Driving a thousand miles with a sad-assed Indian who wouldn't even drink with me hadn't been the high-point of my life. And what had it all been for? So we could sit and stare at a landscape full of nothing.

Finally Norman got out of the car and walked out into the field, which was mostly weeds and where it wasn't weeds was bare ground the same color as the weeds. He wandered around a minute, then started into the same pantomime he'd gone into twenty years ago: waving his arms up and down and stepping off a few paces in one direction and several more in another. I didn't know whether to laugh or get behind the wheel and put the pedal to the metal.

I was about set to do both when this funny feeling came over me. I didn't know what it was. It wasn't Norman, although he was acting nuttier and nuttier, walking a few steps through the weeds as he looked down at his feet, then turning at a right angle and walking a few more steps, then another turn, and so on. He wasn't walking on the same place, not "his" little patch of ground, though, but off to the side of that a little bit.

Well, I'd come this far. I couldn't say he was a whole lot crazier than I was, could I? Might as well join in the fun. I got out of the car and started walking through the weeds toward Norman.

That funny feeling kept getting stronger and stronger. It was something about the land itself. But I just couldn't put my finger on it. When Norman saw me coming up on him, he stopped pacing, pointed down at the ground, and scuffed at something with his heel.

"Here's the front of the house, the living room. It faced west."

I looked down at the ground. By God there was something there, a line of rocks or something. Then I realized what it was. The remains of a foundation. It ran a few feet north and south, then disappeared in the weeds.

"And here—move over, Bobby—is where it met the south wall of the house."

Yes, I saw it.

"The living room would have gone down about this far, then it would have been the bedroom." He walked a few steps along the foundation, then turned left. "And here would have been the east wall of the bedroom about this far, and then the kitchen would have started. Then turn here and this would be the north wall of the kitchen, and then here comes the living room again. It seems so tiny now, it doesn't seem possible that at one time we had twelve, thirteen, fourteen people living here. 'Course Pa enclosed the back porch when I was a little guy, and in the summer four or five of us would sleep out there. Not in the winter, though . . . I didn't get any of the house, but that's all right. My land starts over here, right by the stump. Ma used to cut the heads off chickens on it."

He laughed, but in a choked-up kind of way like he was about ready to cry.

Could it get any better than this? Norman about to flip out, and me with this funny feeling that I couldn't shake. I kept looking around trying to figure out what it was. Then all of a sudden it hit me: Damned if this really wasn't the same place we'd come to twenty years before!

"Hey, Norman, this is the same place, isn't it?" I said.

"Same place? Same place as what?"

"I mean, the same place you brought us to the first time, you know, when you stole the McCandless pickup."

Norman frowned like I was speaking a foreign language.

"Well, yeah, of course it is. I mean, it's my land."

Then he caught on.

"You mean, way back then, you thought . . . ?"

I shrugged. "How was I to know? I mean, come on, all this stuff looks the same."

He looked at me a long time.

"That means that this time, too, you thought . . . you didn't really believe . . ."

He couldn't finish the sentence.

"Hey, man, like I said, how was I to know? Besides, what difference does it make?"

"Well, Bobby, it was my *home*."

"So?"

He stared at me a while. I was beginning to feel uncomfortable.

Then he said, "You know what, Bobby? You need a little land of your own. You need a little something to leave somebody when you're gone."

"Leave to who? And who are you going to leave *yours* too? Who've you got, Norman? Come on, tell me. Who are you to be giving me advice?"

I touched a sore spot there, I guess, because he just sort of crumpled, bent over, then squatted down on his haunches and stayed that way, picking up handfuls of dust and letting it fall through his fingers. And he was crying, too. Not like that Indian in that commercial a few years back with one crystal tear rolling down his noble face but hiccuping and snuffling and snot running, the works.

"You're right. I ain't nobody to give advice. I ain't got nobody. I messed up my whole life. I ain't got nothing but dirt, and if you don't have anybody to leave it to, it don't amount to anything at all."

I left him there. Didn't sneak off or anything, didn't need to because I wasn't afraid of him anymore, like I'd always been just a little bit—the Bowie knife business. But, hell, I hadn't seen that Bowie knife in twenty years. Naw, I just told him it was time to leave, and he told me to go on, he was going to stay where he was. So I left him. Probably after awhile he hitchhiked back into town. Or maybe he laid down and died out there. Who knows? It wasn't any of my business.

I drove back to Springfield and got as much stuff out of my apartment as I could get in my car and left the rest for the landlord, who wasn't going to be too happy about me running out on the lease, but then when are landlords ever happy? I drove to Wichita. Why Wichita? Because I was too tired to drive any farther.

And that's where I've been for the last couple of weeks. I have a new apartment, and I'm working at this water-theme park cleaning up and doing maintenance crap. The job runs out at the end of the summer, but by then I'll probably have run out, too.

I think a lot about Norman. Crazy Indian. I think it'd be a good story to tell somebody in a bar sometime. But I haven't told it yet, even though I do a little bar-hopping every single night. Whenever I'm on the verge of telling the story, something stops me. It's this funny feeling I get. Not the same funny feeling I got out in South Dakota with Norman, but connected to that in a way. What I feel is, I don't know, I feel almost like I envy Norman. I mean, come on now, how in the hell can you explain *that*?

AT THE OLD BALLGAME

Jason and Ryan Tarver, both in their early thirties, had been living with their Grandfather, Jack Bevins, since they lost their jobs at Signage, Inc., over the incident with the line foreman, which had occurred after hours and so might have been of interest to the police, but they were damned if they could see why the Signage brass had to get involved. It'd left a bad taste in their mouths vis-a-vis the whole working thing, and they would have been quite content to stay with Old Jack, as they called him, if he hadn't been so tight with his money. Being a semi-invalid, he didn't have much need of money that they could see, yet every time they came to him for a handout he'd roll over in bed and put his face to the wall and one hand over his hip pocket, although that wasn't where he kept his money. He had it somewhere down in the mattress, they thought, but since he was too ornery to get out of bed while they were around, they hadn't managed to test their theory. One night they decided to go to the ballgame.

In times past the Arkansas Travs had been the best deal in town. It was Double-A ball, and like it as not you'd see a player or three who'd been in the Bigs or soon would be, making millions, face up there on TV. "I saw that guy play right out here at Ray Winder Field not two years ago," you'd say, "and free, too."

Nominally, the games had cost a few dollars, but every single day they'd list a "special promotion" in the paper, free tickets at Mobil or Chuck E. Cheese or Safeway. Only a damn fool ever paid to watch the Travs play. All that's gone now, though, like most good things back in the day. You'll pay five dollars or you'll play hell watching baseball in Little Rock.

Jason and Ryan didn't have five dollars between them.

"Go ask the old man," Jason told Ryan.

"You ask him."

"No, *you* ask him."

Jason was the elder by ten and a half months, and you'd think he'd be the one to take charge, but his idea of taking charge was to get Ryan to do everything. In fact, this generally worked out for the best. When forced to action, Jason too often responded with fists or whatever implement of mayhem was at hand, and as a result he'd seen the inside of the county jail more than once. Ryan, on the other hand, was the thinker of the two, the compromiser if that's what it took, with something of the gift of gab, as in the peroration of his lobbying Old Jack for the ten bucks: "Come on, Old Jack, this isn't just another ballgame. They're tearing down Ray Winder after this season. Yes they are yes they are! You saw it in the paper I know you did! You read every crappin' word in that paper. That's our heritage they're tearing down, Old Jack. Jason and me, we spent the best days of our youth at Ray Winder. Now they gonna build a new ball field across the river in North Little Rock. Probably charge you ten dollars a ticket and ten to park. They'll never see me inside that place. Hell, I wouldn't watch a game in Dog Town if they gave me free tickets and a corn dog to boot."

Old Jack was facing the wall with his hand over his hip pocket. (He wore flannel PJs to bed at night, put on corduroy trousers for his lying in bed in the day.) Without turning back he said, "Who's playing?"

"Jackson," Jason said. He didn't have a way with words like Ryan, but his mind was a sponge for facts like that.

"Jackson, Mississippi?"

"That's where it is unless they moved it."

Old Jack started thrashing around under the covers like a sand crab coming up for air.

"OK, I'll go," he said.

There was a big crowd to see Captain Dynamite blow himself up during the seventh-inning stretch. Combine that with Old Jack being slow getting around, and by the time they got to the field, all the close-in parking spots were taken.

They had to park the old man's Gremlin on the downhill side of the hill north of the ballpark. Old Jack did his best, but he gave out before they even made it to the top of the hill, and they had to half-carry, half-drag him the rest of the way.

"He's a trooper, ain't he?" Ryan would say amiably to anyone who seemed inclined to comment on the proceedings, while Jason, not quite so much the diplomat, would bark, "Keep on staring and somebody'll have to be carrying *your* ass in a minute."

There was an awkward moment at the ticket window as Old Jack struggled to disencumber himself from his grandsons long enough to extract his wallet, stuffed with bills from his stash in his mattress, from his hip pocket. Another when Old Jack's belt caught on the turnstile, and they had to turn him horizontal to get him free. Then up the ramp and down again to the box seats. They picked out an empty box just to the right of the first-base dugout, close as they could get to the boxes occupied by the players' wives, real hotties some of them. Of course they'd only paid for general admission seats, but if the ticket holders showed up, they could always move, or commence the ass-kicking, as the mood took them. It was likely that they'd get thrown out at some point anyway. They'd prefer that it not come too early in the evening, not before they'd had a chance to get through a healthy number of beers, at least. But, hey, a man's gotta do . . .

They propped up Old Jack against the metal bar that separated their box from the next one. They'd take turns sitting next to him, holding on to his sleeve with one hand in case he pitched forward.

Old Jack hadn't said a word since they left the house, and now he sat exactly as they positioned him, still as a mannequin except for his rheumy eyes sliding from right to left, left to right. When they asked him how he was doing, though, his voice was surprisingly strong.

"This is good, this is good. A ballgame! This is good. Thanks, boys."

"Hell, you're paying for it," Jason said.

Old Jack must have misunderstood because he said, "Sure, I played. Hell yes, I did. Third base. Them ground balls, I'd knock 'em down with my chest like Marty Marion. I could hit shit-fire out of the ball, too, except for curve balls. I always thought curve balls was kind of cowardly, in a way."

"I never threw no chicken-shit curve ball," Ryan said.

Ryan pitched some for Hall High his junior year. He could throw it through a brick wall, and, while he couldn't get it anywhere near the plate, he had a real knack for hitting batters. His coach finally figured out that was pretty much his sole intent on the mound and booted him off the team. Still, Ryan looked back on his "athletic career," as he called it, as the golden days.

"Can't picture you playing third, Old Jack," Ryan said, "a tall galoot like you. You're built more like a first baseman, or maybe a pitcher, like me."

At this reference to Ryan's "athletic career," Jason snorted. He'd never played any organized team ball himself because he decided at around age six that he wasn't about to let any son of a bitch tell him how to hold a bat. He was hell on the sandlots, though. Big guy, strong as an ox. Not as big as Old Jack, though.

Jason and Ryan spent a moment or two contemplating the spectacle of their grandfather, all six-foot-four of him, patrolling the hot corner. Then as if by tacit agreement they turned to the more pressing issue.

"Well, Old Jack, 'bout time for a beer, ain't she?"

"Hardly a real ballgame without beer, in my book," Ryan added.

Old Jack seemed to be finished with talking by this point, though. He ignored his grandsons' overtures as he sat slumped against the rail staring out in the general direction of the pitcher, who was in the process of walking the first batter of the game.

"Hey, you're not getting cold there, are you, Old Jack?" Ryan said. He put his arms around Old Jack and vigorously rubbed him up and down, at the end of which maneuver he had the old man's wallet in his hand. He passed it to Jason and winked.

"Beer," Ryan mouthed silently.

It was a great game, balls flying all over and out of the park. By the bottom of the fifth it was 7-6, the Travs up or maybe Jackson, the boys not too clear on that because by then they'd had a lot of beer, a *lot* of beer.

"Gotta shake the dew off my lily," Jason said, struggling to his feet.

"Bring back a couple of cool ones," Ryan said, handing Jason Old Jack's wallet.

"If I'm not back in half an hour, send out a search party."

After attempts to enter a storage area, the ladies, and then the general manager's office, Jason finally located the men's room. The few stalls were all occupied, and the urinals being one long aluminum trough, this presented difficulties for Jason, who, despite his size and choleric temperament, had a bashful bladder. As long as anyone was at the trough at the same time as he was, even standing at the far end, there would be no action on the Jason front. There were a lot of beer drinkers in the crowd that day, so traffic at the urinal was heavy, and Jason was at the trough long enough that he about forgot why he'd come.

Someone came up and stood right next to him, in fact leaned toward him until their shoulders touched. Jason was ready to respond with an elbow to the Adam's apple when . . . "What the hell's taking you so long, man?" It was Ryan.

"What the hell do you mean? I just got here."

"Bullshit. You shouldn't have left me there all alone, man."

There was something in Ryan's voice. He had a funny look on his face.

"What's up, Ryan?"

Ryan shrugged, that way he used to when he was a little kid and he wanted people—his teacher or their old man or something—to stop talking to him because if they kept talking to him he was going to cry.

"I think the old man's dead," Ryan said.

"Granddad?"

"Yeah, I think so."

"Dead?"

"I think so."

"You sure? . . . Dead? Granddad?"

"I'm pretty sure."

"Shee-it."

They went back to the stands, this time choosing the ramp on the far left side, coming up behind the third-base dugout. They stood in the mouth of the ramp peering over at the boxes behind the first-base dugout. The wire screen that protected fans behind home plate from foul balls was in their way, and they couldn't see clearly. Finally, they made him out, slumped in the far right corner of the box where they'd placed him.

"You really think he's dead?" Ryan whispered.

"He's not moving."

By now the game was in the bottom of the sixth, tied up 7-7. They'd watch a little of the game, then peer over at Old Jack.

"What do you think we ought to do?" Ryan said.

Jason jerked his shoulders like the question irritated him. "Captain Dynamite is up in the seventh-inning stretch," he muttered, like he was talking to himself.

This response seemed to satisfy Ryan. They stood there watching the game, occasionally looking over at Old Jack, who had not moved. It seemed to take a long time for the seventh-inning stretch to get there. There was a bases-loaded jam and a couple of pitching changes. Finally, they were swaying back and forth in the mouth of the ramp as they sang along with the crowd, "Take Me Out to the Ballgame." Then Captain Dynamite and his daughter were out on the infield preparing to blow themselves up. Captain Dynamite lay down in a coffin-like box right next to second base. The announcer led the crowd in a countdown from ten. When they got to three, Jason and Ryan looked across at Old Jack.

". . . two, one." BAWHOOMPH!!

Even though they knew it was coming, Jason and Ryan jumped at the explosion, but Old Jack as far as they could tell didn't move a muscle.

"Well, I guess we might as well get out of here," Jason said.

That's what they did.

They went back home—Old Jack's house; they hadn't really had a home since their mom died when they were teenagers. Both said they were hungry as hell, but that was as far as it went. They sat at the kitchen table not quite looking at one another.

Finally Ryan said, "I feel bad—about Granddad, I mean."

As if he'd been waiting for Ryan to say this very thing, Jason immediately shot back, "Hell, we don't have a thing to worry about. There's not a thing to connect him to us. I've got his billfold, remember?" Here Jason half stood and patted his hip pocket. "They won't even know who he is."

"Then how will they identify him?"

"They won't. That's what I'm trying to tell you. They can't pin a thing on us."

Ryan looked away, like he was searching for something over on the stove.

"Then what'll happen with him? How'll Granddad get buried?"

"How the hell should I know? How would he have got buried if he'd died here? The city'll take care of it. That's what we pay our goddamn taxes for, ain't it?"

Jason's voice was rising, getting squeaky like it did when he was about to blow his stack. In fact, he looked furious. He glared across the table at Ryan.

"You blame me," Ryan said, then clenched his eyes and lowered his chin onto his chest like he was trying not to cry.

Jason and Ryan had been into it a few times in the past, sure, but Jason had never been the type of brother who terrorized his younger brother. Now as he watched Ryan trying to get himself under control, he reached out and patted the table. If Ryan's hand had been there, he would have patted that, too.

"Hell, nobody did anything wrong," he said. "The old man just died. Shit happens, you know that."

Ryan opened his eyes again, but he didn't look at Jason. "We shouldn't have left him like that," he said.

"Yeah? Show me the law we broke." *Besides*, he almost added, *our old man left us, so it's all in the family*. But it wasn't the same thing because he and Ryan had breathed a sigh of relief when they saw the last of that drunken son of a bitch. "Anyway, how are they going to connect him to us?"

"I'm not talking about the goddamn law. I'm just saying we could have done things better tonight. We don't always have to be a couple of bums, do we?"

"Speak for yourself."

"I'm speaking for both of us! We shouldn't have left him. He was our granddad!"

Ryan was on his feet, hands balled into fists, almost shouting. Jason leaned back away from him a moment, and then, like an empty sack collapsing, slumped forward. "No, we shouldn't have left him," he said.

With this admission, Ryan's fury seemed suddenly to vanish. He sat back down. "Well, he died doing what he liked best, at least," he said, "and that ain't all bad. I mean, he died at the ol' ball park and everything. He loved baseball, Granddad did."

Jason nodded. "Yessir, he was a hell of a third baseman, too! I remember our old man saying that Granddad about signed a minor league contract only he had to work and support the family."

This was a lie, but it made him feel good to say it, and Ryan nodded enthusiastically as if he remembered their old man saying that, too.

"Can you imagine that big son of a bitch at third base? Man, he must have covered some ground," Ryan said.

"Not . . ." Jason started to say, "Not that you have to cover a lot of ground at third base," because third basemen mostly had to be quick, like Brooks Robinson, Hall of Famer from right here in Little Rock. Even though he didn't finish his thought, the "not" hung in the air between them, and they didn't say anything for a long time. Finally, Ryan said, "You know, they ought to put up a plaque to Granddad right there in Ray Winder Field. Put it out there in center field, you know, like they have all those plaques and monuments and stuff in Yankee Stadium for all the people who died there." He grimaced and shook his head as if even in saying it he knew it would never happen and that it was the most unfair thing in the world that it'd never happen.

"Yeah, yeah, hell yeah!" Jason said.

They didn't look at each other.

Then Jason snapped his fingers. "You know what we ought to do? We ought to go and play a game of catch, right now."

"Oh yeah, oh *yeah*."

"Play some catch for old Granddad."

"Sort of a tribute."

"That's what I'm saying."

"Oh yeah. Hey! You know what? We ought to sneak into Ray Winder Field, play a game of catch right there on the infield."

"You on the mound, me catching."

"Oh hell yeah! This is great, this is great. We really ought to do it."

"For Granddad."

"Oh *yeah*."

They dug their gloves and an old ball out of the closet and jumped into the Gremlin. The game must have just gotten over with because they met a lot of traffic heading away from Ray Winder. They parked in a lot close in, but there were still quite a few people around, so they walked along with the crowd away from the stadium and sat on a concrete bench on the edge of the zoo grounds.

"I wonder how long it takes them to get everybody out and the place cleaned up," Ryan said.

"I don't know. Probably quite a while, but I'll tell you what, I ain't leaving until I have that game of catch."

"Me neither."

Ray Winder holds only a few thousand people, so it didn't take long for the crowd to thin out. Even after the foot traffic had ceased altogether, though, they continued to sit. At one point Jason reared up slightly and said, "My ass is numb," but then he settled back onto the bench. Sometime later, Ryan said, "I wonder . . ." but he left his thought unfinished. Then the big banks of stadium lights, which they could just make out through the trees, went dark.

"Well, I guess that's it," Ryan said.

"We better wait a little longer. Could still be some folks in there."

They waited a little longer. Then Jason stood up and lit a cigarette. After he'd smoked it all the way down, he ground it under his boot. Then he said, "All right, let's go."

They cut across the dark empty parking lots toward the stadium, which they could not yet see for the oaks and sweet gums lining the lots. It wasn't completely dark, though. There were lights of some sort winking through the trees.

They came out of the last line of trees. Across the street was the stadium. Jason put his hand on Ryan's arm. "Will you look at that," he said.

Ryan gaped at the lights rising up above the left field fence. "Why the hell did they leave the scoreboard on?"

"Look at that son of a bitch."

"What the—?"

"Jackson won! Eleven to eight!"

"But the Travs were ahead when we left."

"Hell yeah."

"I swear to God they were."

"You ain't lying."

"Well, damn. That's baseball for you."

"Now you know why I never played the game, never was on no team like you."

"Hell, I wasn't on one long."

"I couldn't've stood it. A damn good hitter goes out two times out of three. That's no fun in my book."

"You want fun? Try pitching. You can throw exactly the pitch you want to throw, exactly the spot you want to throw it, throw the best goddamn pitch in the world, and some skinny one-eyed bastard can swing falling down and bloop it over the infield for a double."

"That's why I hate baseball. It's a game designed to break your heart."

"You said it there."

Ryan placed his hand on his chest and began to knead as if he had a great pain.

They gave that scoreboard one more look of dismay and disgust, and then turned their backs and walked away with the air of men who did not plan to be seen in those parts ever again.

On their way to the Gremlin, they passed a trash receptacle. Jason reared back as if to slam-dunk his glove but then lowered it again to his side and walked on that way, like a man carrying a lunchbox home after a long day's work. When Ryan saw his brother apparently about to throw his ball glove away, he gave his own glove one sorrowful look, then shifted it from his right hand to the crook of his left arm and cradled it there like a newborn bastard baby. But *his* bastard baby.

THE HORSEMEN

I was home for probably an hour before I discovered the horse in the back yard. I'd broken the bad news to my folks about me and Lara, endured the questions and recriminations as long as I could stand it, and then escaped to the newly screened-in back porch, and there was the horse munching on the Canna lilies that grew along the back of the house. I didn't know if eating Canna lilies was good for horses, but I was pretty sure it wasn't good for the lilies.

"I like your new screen room," I said when I went back inside. "Your new colt, too. By the way, it's eating your Canna lilies."

Daddy lunged up from the La-Z-Boy and rushed out back. Mother put her face in her hands. "Ask *him*," she said before I had a chance to say anything. "I'm out of this."

So, a horse. I knew from reading between the lines of Mother's letters that Daddy had been acting strangely, although how could you tell with him? If strange is a person's normal condition, you need a new word.

Mother looked up. "So, what are you going to do about Lara?"

Fortunately at that moment Daddy came back in, laughing bitterly.

"I pay that guy ten bucks for a bale of hay, and Princess Bride eats the *lilies*," he said. "By the way, Scott, Princess Bride is a pony."

"What?"

"You called her a colt, because she's small, I guess. But a colt is a young male horse. A pony is a specific brand of horse."

"Breed."

"What?"

"Breed. You said 'brand' of horse. Horses come in breeds, not brands."

Usually if it's been quite a while since I've been home, it'll take Daddy and me more than an hour to be at each other's throats, but it looked like we'd cut to the chase. In fact, he was getting that puffed-up look on his face like he was ready to explode. Instead, he laughed again.

"You're right. *Breed*. I'd better start getting that straight if I'm going to be a horseman."

"Where'd you get it?" I asked like I'd ask where you got that new tie, like it was the most natural thing in the world.

"Well," he began but stopped when Mother got up and walked out of the den, her face like a—what?—not a storm cloud but like a cloud after it'd already rained and it had nothing left.

Daddy watched her until she was out of sight. Then he looked at me and shook his head.

"She doesn't understand," he said. Then, smiling and winking: "We Posten men are hard on women."

Ouch. I was glad Mother had left or she would have taken that as her cue to get back into the Lara business. But what more was there to say? I just didn't seem to be any good at marriage. Not much good with women in general when you get right down to it, although I do like them and came close to getting married a number of times but fought off the temptation until I met Lara. We were both in our forties by then, and probably for me it was more a matter of, well, better give this thing a try before I get too old for it. I'd always assumed that's the way it was for Lara, too, but I guess it'd meant more to her all along because she's taken the break-up hard. It was an ugly scene. No use staying around and risk a repeat, so here I am, back at the old homestead.

"I got her at the state fair," Daddy said, and for a moment I was confused by the *her*. That's because for some strange reason I've always thought of horses as male. Horses and dogs were male and cats female. I know, stupid, but it was just a notion I got in my head when I was a kid and never quite got over it. (Lara thinks what I never managed to get over was being a kid.)

"Your mother wouldn't go with me, of course—you know her and crowds— but that's OK, I went by myself and had a gay old time," he went on. "Anyway, I was walking through the carnival, and there was this pony ride. Remember those? Four or five ponies walking in a circle, little kids holding on for dear life? You used to love them when you were a kid."

"I was never on a pony, colt, or horse in my life."

"Like hell."

"Have it your way. Go on. You saw a pony ride."

"Right. There were ponies with kids on them going round and round, and staked off to the side was mine. Princess Bride. I asked the guy running the show why she wasn't working, and he said she was taking a break. She's getting old, he says, and one of these days he's going to have to have her put down. So I bought her."

Anybody else telling the story would no doubt have added a bit more detail. His love for horses, maybe, or a discussion with the man about alternatives, maybe something about arguing over the price, the logistics of the whole thing, how he was going to get the horse home. But no. I knew Daddy, and he hadn't left out anything. It'd taken about as long to happen as it took him to describe it. Horse not working. Asks why not. Okay, I'll buy it.

Mother came out of the kitchen and said she was cooking broccoli for dinner and did I want any with my fried chicken. I said no. She smiled like she wanted to come pat me on the head and said, "Still won't eat your veggies, huh?" Then she asked me what I wanted to drink with dinner, and I said that the bottle of wine I'd brought would do for a start.

She returned to the kitchen, and I turned back to Daddy and said, "So, what are you going to do with the horse? It's going to wreck the back yard."

Mother must have been listening because she charged into the den and, face red as if she were absolutely furious, said, "Yes, but let a dog drop one turd on the front lawn, just one turd!"

I was shocked at Mother, a Baptist seven days a week, saying *turd*, but Daddy laughed and laughed. She returned to the kitchen.

The dog thing happened maybe five years ago, right after Daddy retired. Apparently he decided after never caring much about such things to start keeping up the lawn. He had a sprinkler system installed and watered, fertilized, and edged regularly. But there was this neighbor, Carl Owens, who walked his dog past the house, and when it got to Daddy's newly immaculate lawn, it'd "do its business," as Mother called it. Daddy asked Carl not to let the dog do it on his lawn, and Carl said he'd try to watch it, but the next time, there'd be the dog, taking a dump. Finally one day Daddy was on the look out for them, garden hose at the ready. Dog squats, Daddy opens up, gets the dog and Carl, too. Now Carl, who I vaguely remembered, was a little Caspar Milquetoast guy, but he apparently didn't take to getting hosed down, and he charged Daddy. As soon as Carl stepped on our property, Daddy informed me later, that made it legal in The Great State of Arkansas to kill him. Which he tried to do, unsuccessfully, but inflicted enough damage that the police were called in, court case ensued, fine and jail time (suspended), Daddy now with, I suppose, a record. He still seems proud of the whole thing; Mother, not so much.

Daddy sat there grinning. I didn't want to hear any more about that damn dog, so I stood up and said, "Come on, Daddy, let's go look at her."

"You betcha."

He pushed himself up from the La-Z-Boy. He's seventy now, which makes me feel old. What makes me feel older is being forty-nine. A number of years ago before I got married, in a weak moment, I agreed to go to one of those awful family reunion things where I overheard Aunt Opal ask Mother, "When is Scott ever going to settle down?" I wasn't even forty then. What would she say now, me almost fifty and the marriage on the rocks? Not that I care what she or anyone else thinks about me. Probably Lara and all the other women in my life would say not caring is part of my problem. Maybe Mother would say that, too. Do I care what she thinks? Yes. Little boys have to care what their mothers think, don't they?

Daddy and I went out onto the porch. It wasn't quite dark yet. Princess Bride had left the Cannas and was over in the rear corner of the yard by those bushes, never did know what they were called. She was tawny with a darker mane, stubby legs and a low-slung belly. A Shetland pony? I don't know ponies. Don't know bushes. Don't know women. When I get to something I know, I'll have a drink to celebrate.

"So what are you going to do with her?" I asked. "Keep her," he said. "Yeah, but where? You can't keep her here," I said, and he said, pointing emphatically downward, "Right here."

I told him he couldn't do that because there were zoning laws against it. He said not true, a neighbor only a couple houses down had chickens, and if I got up earlier enough next morning I'd probably hear the sons of bitches clucking away. I was about to tell him he was crazy when I recalled Mother mentioning in a letter (she wrote me every week, and sometimes I wrote back) that Daddy had called the police on a neighbor who had chickens.

"Chickens are one thing," I said. "Horses are another kettle of fish."

"Chickens, horses, fish. You get two of each and you can start your own ark. Then all you'll have to find is a woman to sail off with and you'll be all set for the next flood."

"As long as I don't have to marry her," I said, and he came back with, "Hell, that'll be no problem for you. You can always divorce her as soon as the rain stops."

Somewhere in there we'd gone from joking to not joking. This happens with us, all right. Mother says we're too much alike, but that's a load of crap. Women aren't always right about us men, not even mothers.

While I was trying to think of an appropriately cutting rejoinder, Mother came around from the side of the house and said to Daddy, "John, the propane tank on the grill is dry. Run down to 7-Eleven and get a refill."

"I thought you were frying the chicken, Mother," I said. They keep the gas grill on the side of the house, but I don't remember Mother ever using it. Grilling is a man thing, right?

"When you said you wouldn't eat broccoli, I decided to grill. I'll grill some roasting ears, too. You like those."

I smiled at her "roasting ears." She and her family are the only people I know who call corn on the cob that. They're hill people. Mother still thinks Little Rock is a big city.

Daddy said something about having to go out this time of night but then said, "Aw hell, okay," and went out the screen door and around to the side of the house, where I heard him fiddling with the propane tank. Did I hear him whistling? Could be he wasn't all that sorry to get out of the house for a bit. After all, I'd already been home for over an hour. An hour of me is about all he can take. Well, right back at you, Pop.

Pop. I never called him that, though. It's Mother and Daddy. A Southern thing. It used to be the *daddy* that embarrassed me if I slipped and called my father that when talking to someone from Oregon, or California, where I lived before meeting Lara. Now, though, it's *mother* that sounds stranger to my ear, that curious formality, son to mama.

She stood there on the other side of the screen, face barely recognizable in the gathering darkness, but I could tell by her profile that she wasn't looking at me but back toward the side of the house where the grill was, waiting, I'd bet, for Daddy to get out of earshot.

Then she turned to me and said, "You've got to get *rid* of it."

"Get rid of what?" I said although of course I knew. She didn't bother answering but repeated, "You've got to get rid of it *now*. I can't take it, Scott. I just can't take the childishness anymore."

Her voice broke over *childishness*, and I held my hands up, surrendering, and said, "Okay, Mother, don't worry. I'll think of something."

At that moment, from somewhere in the house Daddy sang out, "Home, home on the range!" And then he bellowed out a long laugh. I thought I heard the garage door open, then close. I exhaled. I hadn't realized I'd been holding my breath.

I stood almost within touching distance of Princess Bride. It'd taken a while for me to force myself that close. Mother was behind me, over by the screen door of the porch. I looked back at her.

"Go on," she said. "Speak softly to her. Get her confidence."

"Sweetheart. Beauty. Oh, my precious baby," I said. Princess Bride stood there.

"Maybe pat her. Run your hand over her, gently," Mother said.

No, I was not going to run my hand over her. We didn't have that kind of relationship. But I did summon the courage to edge a step closer and give her a pat on the neck. A shiver ran the length of her body. She seemed as scared as I was. I felt sorry for her, taken from her home, in this unfamiliar place now, and in the hands of strange men. Posten men, at that.

"It's okay, honey, it's okay," I murmured and gave her a couple more pats, left my palm resting on her neck. I could feel the blood pulsing, but the trembling had stopped. But this wasn't getting us anywhere. I looked back at Mother.

"Give her mane a tug."

I took a handful of her long dark hair (black or brown, I couldn't tell) and gave it a little pull; to my surprise Princess Bride did take a few steps into the middle of the yard, but then she stopped and didn't respond to further tugs.

"Get on her," Mother said. "She's used to being ridden."

"You are of course kidding."

"What are you afraid of? You're bigger than she is. Just get on her and ride her off our property. You can take her down to the park and let her loose. Or just let her loose on the street. Somebody's bound to call the police eventually, and they can take charge of her."

Actually that wasn't a bad plan. I guarantee you that Daddy didn't have anything as formal as a bill of sale. Chances were no one could trace that horse to us. And if they did, so what? All I was doing was appeasing Mother, anyway. Once the horse was gone, I'd wash my hands of the whole thing, and Mother and Daddy could fight it out. They were good at that.

I looked at Princess Bride. Mother was right, I was bigger than her. Taller, anyway. I'm six-four, and if I ever got up on her, my feet would probably drag on the ground.

Get up on her? What was I thinking?

Before I lost what little courage I had, I threw a leg over her, sort of lunged and rolled, and then somehow I was up on her. It obviously helped that she was used to riders. She hadn't so much as flinched. Immediately, in fact, she took a couple of tentative steps, and I felt myself teeter left and then right and desperately wanted something to hold on to, but there was nothing but her neck. I clutched it with both hands.

"I'll get the gate!" Mother called out, and she took off into the house. She'd have to go through the house and then out the attached garage to the gate in the privacy fence that opened onto the front yard, which was always padlocked from the outside.

Princess Bride took another couple of steps, and I was still atop her, so I started to think that this might be doable. But then she turned to the left.

"Not that way, Sweetheart," I said, but she kept turning to the left. We were going back toward the bushes. Now left again and back toward the house.

Then I got it. Of course, she was going in a circle. How did you make her go straight? I tried pushing my left knee against her to nudge her to the right but lost my balance and almost fell off. I tried patting the right side of her neck. Tried giving her mane a tug to the right. Princess Bride circled left.

As we circled back to the house, we passed the window to my bedroom. For an instant I saw a face staring out at me disapprovingly, and I wondered why Mother was in there instead of out here helping. Maybe the humiliation was too much for her. I sympathized. On the next circuit, though, as we passed the window I looked at the face and saw that it wasn't Mother but my own reflection. The humiliation should have been the giveaway.

Still, I have to admit it wasn't totally unpleasant. I was no longer afraid of falling off. Princess Bride, gentle with me as if sensing it was my first time, stepped slowly, swayed gently, the summer night soft and warm and still. But after another circuit she began to slow even more, then after a couple of halting steps stopped, and her head hung down, a shudder running through her with each rasping breath.

I gave her a moment to recover, then lifted my legs at her sides and brought my heels down against her ribs. "Giddy up!" I commanded. Without lifting her head, she began to move.

RAG AND BONE

The last time Jon had invited someone home to dinner without his wife, Toni, nagging him into it was, well, never. She stood staring at him for several seconds after he broke the news to her. Then she said, "What is he—a divorce attorney?"

Things had been rocky between Jon and Toni for a long time.

"His name's Allen Pratt," Jon said. "He's a poet."

"Oh, one of those," Toni snorted. "You've had poets in town before. You've never invited one to dinner yet. Why this guy?"

"I'm not exactly sure how it happened myself," Jon said. "He showed up at my office this morning and—"

Toni broke in: "You mean someone actually found you in the crypt?"

Jon's office at the university was located in a tiny, run-down bungalow on a cul-de-sac a block from the main campus. It was hard for students and administrators to find—its chief attraction for Jon, who claimed to need the extra room for *Foul Rag*, the literary journal he'd been editing for over a decade now.

Somehow, though, he told Toni, Allen Pratt had found him this morning. They were five minutes into the conversation before Jon figured out that Allen wasn't some new associate dean come to check up on him. Finally, the guy's name rang a bell. Allen Pratt had been sending Jon five poems an issue—five in the spring, five in the fall—for as long as Jon could remember. A few months ago, out of pity or fatigue or maybe because something had actually risen above that sea of mediocrity to the level of the almost readable, Jon had accepted one of the poems for Foul Rag. Now the kicker: Allen had driven all the way from Adrian, Michigan, to be on the scene when the issue with his poem came out! Jon's assurance that it could be three or four more weeks before it was back from the printers didn't faze him in the least. Allen said he wasn't wealthy, but he hadn't had a vacation since his wife died. He could use some time off. Yeah, but in Forrest City, Arkansas? Jon felt sorry enough for the poor sap that he'd invited him to dinner—fully expecting him to refuse, of course. Lamentably, Allen had accepted.

Toni shook her head. "He seems to be about as big a nutcase as you are."

"What the hell does that mean?"

Toni ignored him and began thumbing through recipe books. She was humming to herself, some tune Jon almost recognized. Her eyes were shining. She was going to get to entertain! Jon shook his head. Funny how little it took, sometimes, to make a woman happy.

Allen arrived carrying a small bouquet of flowers for Toni. To Jon they looked suspiciously like they'd been pilfered from someone's lawn, But Toni was tickled pink with them. How little it took . . .

Jon would have preferred that Allen had brought a nice bottle of wine, preferably a big red to kill the taste of whatever Toni was preparing for dinner. She'd been known to commit atrocities on the range. Jon did most of the cooking, in fact, except for those rare occasions when they had guests, at which point Toni insisted on taking over, flitting about the kitchen nervously and earnestly, desperate to please. Back in their happier days, Jon had thought it was cute.

While Toni finished up the cooking, Jon and Allen sat in the den munching on a store-bought cheese ball and crackers as Jon struggled and generally failed to make small talk. Allen didn't help much. He'd been ebullient at the office earlier in the day but now was much more reserved, and he seemed especially deflated by the news that he wouldn't get to meet Jon and Toni's children, whom he'd mistakenly inferred still lived at home. "Naw, thank God I got those bastards off my hands years ago," Jon laughed, but Allen didn't seem to see the humor in the comment. At that moment, Toni stuck her head in the den and glared furiously at Jon, as if she'd been waiting with her ear pressed to the door for just such a contretemps.

Things got a little better once they went in to dinner. As the other two chatted, Jon was able to concentrate his attentions on the Australian Shiraz he'd popped, Toni limiting herself to her usual single glass while Allen stuck to water.

The festivities broke up before nine, no great damage done to anyone. Allen thanked them for a lovely evening, and Jon thanked God it had lasted no longer.

Jon helped Toni clean up the dishes.

"He's a very, very sad man," Toni said as she dreamily polished and polished and polished a dinner plate.

"Hey, the lucky devil has a poem coming out in *Foul Rag*. What's he got to be sad about?"

"Hm, could it be because his wife's dead? *Duh*."

"Somehow I got the impression she'd been dead a good while."

"Friday it'll be ten years ago to the day that she died. Didn't you hear him say that?"

"Right, right."

"He was sort of hoping the poem would come out on that day."

Jon let the pot he was scrubbing fall back into the sink. "Say what? You mean on Friday to the day? But that's crazy."

"He knows that. He knows it's crazy. Didn't you hear anything the man said? That's why the man's so sad. He *knows* it."

Jon turned back to the sink, shaking his head. "Yeah, well, ten years. It's time ol' Al was moving on."

"Ol' Al must have loved his wife very much."

"Nevertheless . . ."

Toni went straight to bed after they were done in the kitchen. By the time Jon finished reading the paper and doing the crossword puzzle—got every single one!—then watched the news and Dave Letterman's monologue, he expected Toni to be asleep, but he found her lying there staring up at the ceiling. She seemed lost in thought—about poor ol' Al, Jon bet.

But Toni surprised him by saying, "You never said a word about my chicken cacciatore."

"Didn't I? I thought it was damn good."

"Yeah, right. Now you say it after I have to bring it up myself. It would have been polite to have mentioned it earlier. A little courtesy's a good start, you know."

A good start toward *what*, he almost asked. But he kept his mouth shut.

He undressed, brushed his teeth, and got into bed. They used to sleep in a standard, but a few years ago they'd purchased a king-size bed. With the independent-coil suspension, one could do all the moving around he wanted, and the other would hardly know anyone else was in bed.

He took the Fagles translation of *The Odyssey* from the nightstand and had just located his place when Toni said, "Sydney got her body pierced."

Jon slammed the book down. "What?"

Sydney was their unmarried daughter. She'd moved out of the house a year ago.

"She called me today and told me. She got her body pierced. She had a ring inserted."

Jon thought a minute. "Where?"

"I think there's a place at the mall where they do it."

"No, goddamn it, I mean where on her body?"

"I promised Sydney I wouldn't tell you," Toni said. "Anyway, you can't see it when she's dressed."

"I bet that goddamn Aaron Staley knows where it is."

"I hope so. They're living together, after all."

Toni turned off her light.

Jon tried to read. He read the same passage over and over. The words made no sense.

Suddenly, Toni sat up and declared, "If I was a young girl today, I'd get my body pierced everyplace! I'd have rings and rings and rings just everywhere!"

Then she flopped back down and turned her back to him.

Jon lay there for some minutes, the book on his chest, trying to figure out what the hell was going on. Then he gave up on it and turned the light off. He never slept well. That old gambit, counting sheep, sometimes helped, but generally not before he'd exhausted himself tossing and turning for an hour or two. Tonight, he tried it immediately. The eleventh sheep had just glided over the little wooden fence when Toni's voice came out of the darkness: "You used to say I hung the stars."

Jon thought a minute. "I believe the expression is 'hung the *moon*,'" he said.

After his morning classes the next day, Jon went back to his office and started in on his PB & J and Diet Coke. He'd half expected to find Allen waiting on his doorstep, but there was no sign of him. What was the poor schmuck doing with his time today, Jon wondered.

He put his sandwich down, went over to a filing cabinet, and took out the manila folder containing the manuscripts for the fall issue of *Foul Rag*. Thumbed through until he found Allen's submission: "This Poem."

The irksome title jogged his memory. It was indeed the best of the poems Allen had sent him over the years, but that was the faintest of praise. Jon gave it a rapid read-through. A lot of feeling, very little art. Jon would have preferred the opposite. It concerned the death of his wife, Misty. God-awful name. Jon had almost phoned Allen asking him to change it but couldn't work up the energy. Almost changed it himself but didn't have the nerve. The last three lines—

> Once I had Misty.
>
> Then I had grief.
>
> Now only this poem.

—Jon found borderline interesting but problematic. The rest of the poem had been unrhymed free verse, but those last three lines seemed to beg for a fourth to rhyme with "grief."

> I can't get no relief . . .
>
> Time is the thief . . .
>
> Where is the beef? . . .

Jon snickered. He liked that last one a *lot*. He wondered how many of his students were old enough to get the allusion. Damn few. Yes, time is indeed the thief.

He glanced at the poem again. "Ten years now . . ." Echoes of Wordsworth, "Tintern Abbey."

Toni had said something about the tenth anniversary of the death of Allen's wife in a day or two. So Allen had written the poem—Jon received it last spring—with that anniversary in mind. With, perhaps, being here, in Forrest City, Arkansas, right now, in mind. Strange, strange. Crazy!

Jon returned the folder to the filing cabinet, then stood there looking at the rank of filing cabinets lined up along the wall like squat gray-uniformed soldiers. He bet he had more filing cabinets than any other professor at the university. Over the years he'd saved the cover letter of each and every submission, with "accepted" or, much more frequently, a big circled "NO" and date of same scrawled across it.

Those babies could come in handy, had already come in handy when a new, hired-from-outside department head questioned Jon's release time for editing *Foul Rag*. Jon mounted his defense by quite literally carting over seven years of cover letters to prove how much work was involved even in opening two to three thousand manuscripts a year. Case closed!

Jon went back to the earliest dates in the files and began searching through the cover letters. He finally found the cover letter for Allen's first submissions, citing five poems by title. Big circled NO like a brand burnt onto it. Date.

The submissions would have been for *Foul Rag*'s second issue. Until that moment, Jon hadn't realized that the tenth anniversary of *Foul Rag*'s acquisition by Jon and Arkansas Delta University had passed an issue ago. It would have been middling interesting—a "fearful symmetry" of sorts?—if Allen's ten years of submissions had coincided with the journal's ten-year existence in its present incarnation. Life's symmetries were a good deal more lopsided than art's, though. Still, only one issue off.

Allen must have seen that first issue, then submitted. Yes, there it was.

Jon closed the filing cabinet. Wait, though. Was that the explanation? No, of course not. Allen's wife died, and then he started to write poetry. There was the symmetry. *Foul Rag*, Jon himself, were incidental features of the equation.

Once I had Misty.

Then I had grief.

Now only this poem.

Jon shook his head. No, still not right. Something missing. But maybe that had been Allen's point all along.

Jon had a hunch that Allen would be there waiting for him when he returned home that afternoon, but his hunch was wrong. No sign of him next morning at the office, either. Jon felt an urge to go looking for him—why, he couldn't say. Maybe it was that almost-symmetry. But he did nothing.

The call came a little after noon. Allen's voice was shaking, his breath came in shallow, rasping jerks. He'd been in a car wreck.

"Where are you?" Jon said.

Allen was at a Mobil station out on the highway.

"I'll be there in ten minutes."

By the time Jon pulled into the station, Allen still hadn't gotten himself under control. He looked as if he might have been crying. His car, a Ford Escort that looked like it had seen better days even before the accident, was sitting on the wrecker bed behind the station.

"It's totaled. Totaled. Totally totaled," Allen said.

"What happened?"

"There was a ball. A soccer ball, I think," Allen said. He gestured vaguely in the direction of the access road. "It rolled across the road."

Jon frowned. "A ball rolled across the road? Was a kid chasing it or something?"

Allen didn't remember seeing any child. Just the ball. Soccer ball, he thought. It rolled across the road in front of him and he swerved and hit a culvert. The car was totaled.

"My wife died of cancer. It took three months from the day she was diagnosed. Now I'm fucked by a goddamn soccer ball," Allen said.

Jon was shocked by the foul language. Allen didn't seem the type—*prim* almost. But now the mask was off, maybe.

Jon said, "Well, at least you're all right. That's the important thing."

"Bullshit. I need the car. I was on my way out of town, heading back to Michigan, when it happened."

"I thought you intended to stay here until the fall issue comes out."

"Can't. Have to be back tomorrow. Tomorrow is the anniversary."

"I know, but . . . ." Jon gave up on it. Nothing Allen did made any sense to him.

"Look, Allen," he said, "you can just make a call to your insurance agent, get the paperwork rolling, then take a flight back to Michigan. There's plenty of time."

Allen shook his head. "Can't. Can't fly."

"Why not?"

"Can't afford it."

Jon was taken aback. "What do you mean, you can't afford it? You have enough money for a three or four week stay here but not enough—"

"I have no money," Allen said. "I've been sleeping in my car. I bought a loaf of bread and a jar of peanut butter at the store. I clean up at gas stations. I used to be a comptroller at our local newspaper, but I drank myself out of that job five years ago. Haven't held a job for more than two or three months at a time since then. I've got nothing."

Jon didn't know what to say. Allen looked off down the road, his eyes whipping left and right as if he were desperately searching for something. Maybe that soccer ball.

"You better come home with me," Jon said finally.

"OK," Allen said, without enthusiasm.

Jon had just gotten Allen into the house when Toni pulled into the drive. She worked half-days as an in-home-care nurse.

Jon met her in the garage and gave her the short version of Allen's woes.

"You take him," she said almost before Jon had finished.

She glared at him as if ready for a fight.

"Well, actually," he said, "I did think about helping the poor guy out a little. Maybe lending him the money for a plane ticket. Not that there's much chance we'd ever get it back."

"No. You take him. You drive him back."

"But why?"

"Because he doesn't need to be alone now. Besides, he came all this way to see you."

Jon canted his head and said with a smirk, "Boy, you'll try anything to get rid of me, won't you? What, got some guy you're playing around with or something?"

Toni took a step back like he'd spat at her. "You know, you're rude. You're just rude. And no, I'm not seeing anyone. It'd be enough just having you out of the house for a couple of days."

Jon tried to hold the smirk, but it was no good. He felt his face twist and then freeze into—what? He didn't know. He wished he had a mirror so he could see what his face looked like. Then maybe he'd know what he was feeling

Jon didn't bother calling the department chair with some excuse for his being gone Friday. They were used to not seeing Jon around.

Jon and Allen left in the late afternoon and drove through the night. Jon kept himself awake with massive amounts of coffee and the dubious pleasures of talk radio. Allen didn't volunteer to help with the driving. He didn't volunteer much at all, in fact, hardly speaking until Jon, who'd been careful to avoid the subject until then, mentioned "This Poem," which of course brought up Jon's life with Misty, and without her. It was all right there in those last three lines of the poem. Misty had been his whole life. They'd never had children. After she died he'd turned to poetry—always an interest of his, but he'd never had the time for it. Now all he had was time. All the poems were about Misty in one way or another, about her and his grief. The grief had been so terrible that for years he wasn't sure he could go on living. Maybe the poetry was what kept him going. At a certain point, though, he realize that he'd written it all to death—love, Misty, and grief—and that all he was left with were the words.

"That's why I came to Arkansas, to be there when the poem came out. There it would be, I'd see it, hold it. If it's enough, I go on. If not . . ."

They drove on. Jon didn't hear a peep out of Allen for a long time. He thought he must have dropped off to sleep.

But then: "So what do you think?"

"What do I think about what?" Jon said.

"About somebody's chances of living just for words."

"How should I know?"

"Well, you seem to be pretty involved with your editing."

Jon snorted. "I don't give a crap about editing."

That was it for the chit-chat. They pulled into Adrian mid-morning.

"So? Where to now?" Jon asked.

Allen smiled ruefully. "Well, I'm locked out of my apartment—been a little while since I paid the rent. So that's no good. Hell, just take me to the cemetery."

At the cemetery Allen had to ask the caretaker for directions to Misty's grave. "First time I've been here since the funeral," he explained to Jon. "I told myself that all this didn't matter. It was just dirt and grass and a hole in the ground. But I think I was afraid I wouldn't be able to stand it."

Jon hung back as they neared the grave, but Allen waved him on.

"You've come this far. And don't worry, I'm not going to go off the deep end. Wish I could, but I've got nothing left in here," he said, tapping his chest with his fist. "Words words words—that's all. Hollow men don't go off the deep end."

They stood in front of the grave.

"Petrarch . . . You remember Petrarch, at Laura's grave, those sonnets? Hell now, if I could do that, there would be some poems for you."

Allen was evidently trying to smile ironically or sarcastically or archly—something—as he spoke of Petrarch, but that ludicrous grimace was no smile. Horrible the look, horrible.

"Or perhaps I should be speaking of Henry James now. 'The Beast in the Jungle'? Good ol' Marcher standing by May's grave, feeling nothing, hollow as—"

Jon cut him off: "Allen! What are you babbling about? Stop it! You keep saying you don't feel anything. My God, man, who do you think you're kidding? You should see your face, man. You should look in a mirror. Not feel anything? Hell, man, you're in *hell*."

Allen stood there working his mouth like something was stuck in his throat.

"Allen," Jon said, very gently this time, "if all you care about now are the poems, then why are you *here*?"

Allen closed his eyes and turned his face as if someone were about to slap him.

The sun glowed weakly behind a thin overcast of cloud. A stiff breeze pushed Jon's trousers against his legs.

Finally Jon said, "Allen, you can't stand here forever. What are you going to do now? Where can I take you? Family? Friends? There must be someone. . . . OK, then, OK. You're coming home with me. We have an extra room. You can stay with us until you get back on your feet, decide something."

Allen said nothing.

Jon stood there a bit longer. Then he reached into his wallet, took out his cash and, save for one twenty, stuffed it all in Allen's pocket.

"I have to go," he said.

When he got home, he'd tell Toni that Allen was grateful for the money, that he said he'd turned a corner now, he had a future, was going to get back on his feet. But in fact Allen had said not another word, and Jon had left him still standing at the foot of Misty's grave.

Jon headed straight back, fighting sleep all the way. Coffee didn't help. In fact, he napped several times on gas station parking lots and slept for over three hours at a rest stop outside of Bowling Green, Kentucky, until he woke up cold and stiff and headachy.

He felt better driving across Arkansas, though, a cool, sunny, soft October morning. Coming into Forrest City was strange. He'd been gone less that thirty-six hours, but he felt like he was returning to some place from his distant past, a childhood home, maybe, a place of which he had fond memories.

He parked in front of his house, walked across the lawn, and rang the doorbell. He was a bit disoriented from his travels and couldn't think whether Toni should be home or not. But in a moment she came to the door. She looked surprised when she saw it was him. Then puzzled.

"What are you doing?" she said.

"What do you mean?" he said.

"Why are you ringing the bell? Your key's in your hand."

He let out a little bark of laughter. "Oh yeah, right, I forgot. I just . . . It's been a long couple of days."

They stood there a moment looking at one another, and then Jon said, "May I come in?"

TO THE FORDYCE BATHHOUSE

There's something of the aging whore in Hot Springs, Arkansas. So desperate to please, forever applying garish makeup to a body long ago gone to seed. It was there that Bill Clinton came of age and, one scalding summer fifty years ago, I did not. And now I have come back. Why? To retrace that path my mother and I walked every afternoon from Levi Hospital, rising surreally above one end of decaying Bathhouse Row, to dowdy, majestic Arlington Hotel standing watch over the other. To walk that path and recall it to memory, all of it, to see it clearly and understand, as much as it will no doubt hurt, where we went wrong, my mother and I, with each other and the world. It is too late to repair the damage with my mother; the dead may return to haunt but not to forgive. But what of the world? I return to Hot Springs to find someone in the wide world to love me, and me to love.

We lived in an apartment on Opera Street, a few blocks up from Central Avenue where the bathhouses stood shoulder to shoulder in fading grandeur, their best years behind them. Our apartment was little better, actually the walk-in basement of a one-story clapboard bungalow owned by a couple—the Whittiers—I thought of as ancient. (They were probably in their fifties.) There was a tiny refrigerator that wheezed like an asthmatic and a hot plate for cooking. The floor was concrete and rugless with the shadow of an oil stain in the middle of our bedroom/living room. I think it must have been a garage in a previous life. Running from floor to ceiling in the wall behind the sleeper-sofa was a crack wide enough, if you canted your head just right, to see daylight through. But, the basement being cut out of the side of a hill so that half of it was underground, it was cooler than anywhere else except the air-conditioned lobby of the Arlington Hotel, that summer of 1957. Cooler, and we didn't live there long enough for me to tire of suppers of boiled hot dogs or tins of tuna or cans of Campbell's soup. I thought of it as a sort of adventure. I didn't realize we were poor. That wasn't all I didn't realize that summer.

I have come back to Hot Springs, but not to the house on Opera Street. Today, Opera Street is mostly businesses and parking lots. It was better in the old days, I think. (Ach! I sound like an old man. And—sixty now—I suppose I am.)

Among the many things I did not understand about that summer is why we were there. We moved to Hot Springs almost immediately after my last day of school in early June, and we were back in Little Rock in time for me to begin school again in early September, so I assumed the intent had been a three-month summer vacation. Now, though, I realize that surely wasn't the case. It was hardly a vacation for my mother, for one thing. She worked from eight until five Monday through Friday on the custodial staff at Levi Hospital and then put in another hour at the Arlington Hotel afterward. It couldn't have been much fun for her even if I thought of it as something of a lark. So why would she have gone through all that—drudgery, poverty, a dark, cramped, musty basement apartment, speaking in hushed voices so as not to disturb the high and mighty Whittiers above us (even though it was their endlessly playing Patsy Cline and Eddy Arnold records at full volume that drove us to distraction)—just for a three months' change of pace? She wouldn't. No, she hadn't come to Hot Springs for a change of pace; she'd come to change her life. And then she returned to Little Rock because she'd failed. (And where will I go if I fail?)

Oh, the contrast between the apartment on Opera Street and where I lay me head today: a condo on a hillside above Lake Hamilton on the southern edge of the city. Air-conditioning, microwave, frig with ice-maker and cold-water dispenser, convection oven, wall-to-wall carpeting, balcony overlooking the lake, floor-to-ceiling mirrored closet doors overlooking my bed. Overlooking my king-size, empty bed. I, who came here for love.

But why did my mother come here fifty years ago? She would have had to quit her job in Little Rock, find one in Hot Springs and then, when things didn't work out, quit that one and find another back in Little Rock. I told Lucy, my one friend that summer, that my mother was a doctor at Levi Hospital and that she saved people's lives. Ungrateful little prig that I was, I was ashamed to say what she really was: a cleaning lady. We didn't live well, but that we lived at all was due to her. And she had to pay a woman to watch me during the day, too: Mrs. Claycomb, mother of the beauteous Lucy. Every afternoon at 4:50 we'd begin the short trek over to Levi Hospital where I'd be turned over to my mother, and then she and I would walk the path snaking along the hillside between the hospital and Arlington Hotel, where my mother would put in another hour while I sat in a big overstuffed chair in the lobby ("Be a little gentleman, now, Johnny") and dreamed of hunting tigers among the monkeys and parrots, the curling vines and langorous flowers of the jungle-scene mural that so memorably graced the lobby walls. The murals, in fact, are still there. So, in fact, am I.

Today one can book a weekend at the Arlington online, including a thermal bath and massage and a fabulous Sunday brunch of lox and bagels, waffles, and made-to-order omelets. With my $3,000-a-month condo, I do not need (and on my college professor's salary cannot afford) a room in the Arlington, but I've dropped in more than once this summer to gaze at those murals. Also, once this summer, I've partaken of that Sunday brunch. We never ate at the Arlington in 1957, believe me. On this occasion, for once I was not alone. Her name was Karen Goodpasture. We met in early June, not long after I'd moved into the condo, at a "concert in the park," one of those affairs meant to evoke a bygone era, in this case a Currier-and-Ives gay '90s, I suppose. They appeal mostly to the older folks, of which, alas, I am one. Karen, too, although she's maybe a decade younger than I. I don't have much of the gift of gab, and "picking up" a woman is not something I'm much good at. But it was one of those soft late-spring evenings, and the music was as good as a bottle of wine for putting one in the mood, and I found myself beside this not unattractive woman, and then we were talking. The next Sunday we were sharing brunch at the Arlington, and not many nights after that she was in my bed in the condo, on her side facing me, her auburn hair (natural!) iridescent against her pearly white skin, eyes blue, breasts not sagging nearly so much as one as unkind as I might expect. She looked at me invitingly, then looked away shyly as a fifty year old will on the verge of love for the first time in a long, long while. And that was what I'd come for, wasn't it—twice-divorced, childless, one last chance at love before the long implacable lonely descent? I looked at her, fondly and desirously, I truly think, but then glanced at her reflection in those goddamned mirrored closet doors behind her, and there it was: her puckered ass, and the varicose veins at the backs of her knees, and her orange-callused heels. At that moment she looked up and saw me looking and guessed what I was thinking. And so it was over before it began. And I regret it. I had come for love, and Karen was a nice woman. But there was that puckered ass, and a puckered ass, once seen, cannot be unseen.

✳

I was afraid of Levi Hospital. It was too large, for one thing. It loomed above one so, an inscrutable monolith, an eyeless god, and I was so small (at age ten, two years from puberty, so small that, sitting in the huge, delightfully cool leather chair in the lobby of the Arlington Hotel, waiting for my mother to finish her extra hour of work so we could go "home" and eat our boiled hot dogs, our tins of tuna, my feet did not quite touch the floor). I loved the Arlington. The people there, I was certain, were rich and carefree, and I pretended we were rich along with them. The people in Levi Hospital, though, oh, I feared them. I think its specialty must have been muscular diseases and the like because so many of the patients were in wheelchairs and on crutches, their faces scarred with pain and weariness and despair. I had the notion they came in whole and it was the hospital that maimed them. I was afraid it'd do the same to my mother. I was afraid it'd do the same to me. After Mrs. Claycomb and Lucy turned me over to my mother every afternoon at five, we'd walk off hand in hand toward the Arlington, and half a dozen times before we got there I'd look back and there Levi Hospital would always be, rising above the trees, above everything. It's still there on Reserve Street, looming over Central Avenue and Bathhouse Row, and me. And I still fear it.

⁂

Life is fraught with surprising symmetries. Levi Hospital rising up out of the side of the hill above Central Avenue; the Arlington Hotel rising up out of the same hill; the basement apartment in the Whittiers' house on Opera Street cut out of the side of a hill; my condo, on the far south end of Central Avenue, cut out of the side of the hill overlooking Lake Hamilton, its shores studded with restaurants and boat docks and million-dollar summer homes. I sit on my balcony sipping Earl Grey and gaze across at Big Al's Marina on the opposite side of this arm of the lake. Souvenirs. Cold Beer and Hot Hotdogs. Fishing Licenses Sold. Boat Rentals. Jet Ski Rentals. The Jet Skis are especially popular this summer with the young men and their young women in their bikinis, all tanned and bodies slick and gleaming, with sunscreen, I suppose. Or maybe just sweat. They love the Jet Skis, the young women. How they squeal as they spread their legs and mount them. The shirtless fellow who works the dock shows them just how to position their feet and where to put their hands. When the motor throbs to life, I can almost see from here how their eyes roll back in their heads. Can they possibly imagine how much they disgust me? Yes, yes, symmetries beset me, and all of them meaningless.

⁂

I suppose I was a little in love with Lucy Claycomb that summer. I was ten years old and she a little younger, but she led me around by the nose, and I was happy to be led. I think of her as being "cute as a bug's ear"—(did my mother call her that?)—but I cannot see her clearly now. Blue eyes, I think, and blonde hair. Ringlets? Or was that from a Shirley Temple movie? The Claycombs had a television (my mother and I were too poor for one, of course), and every afternoon we watched *Howdy Doody*. I called Lucy Princess SummerFallWinterSpring, and she called me Howdy—unless I failed to obey her every whim, and then it was Mr. Bluster. She almost never had to call me Mr. Bluster. We played hopscotch on the sidewalk and a limited form of hide 'n' seek, not being allowed to go beyond the confines of the Claycombs' property. We played "doctor"—or rather "nurse" with Lucy's pink plastic nurse's kit. She was the one in the paper nurse's cap—and I was the one with the plastic thermometer in his mouth. I told Lucy my mother was a doctor at Levi Hospital, but I don't think she believed me. I was the naïve one. It was a summer of love, 1957, or as close to it as I ever got. When we left Hot Springs that August, I cried. So did my mother. I thought it was because she'd lost her job at the Arlington because a man I'd see once or twice at the hotel came by our apartment and there was a scene of some kind. I didn't understand anything.

⁂

I keep an eye out for Karen Goodpasture. I've been back to three or four of those concerts in the park, but no luck. She lives on Garden Street, but I don't know the exact address and her name isn't in the phone book. (We always met someplace on our few dates; I never picked her up at her house. Perhaps she wanted to keep her address to herself until she found out whether I was a bastard or not. Well, she found out.) Hot Springs is a very small city. You'd think I'd run into her by accident at some point. And I'd like to do that, get a second chance, even if I'm not really sure what I'd say or do. Apologize, I suppose, but for what, exactly? A look on my face? Seeing the truth? I'd like to tell her, *Look, let's forget all that stuff—the body and all that. The body's not important.* But something tells me that's not what she'd want to hear. Oh, the vanity of women. The only thing worse is the vanity of men! I look at myself in those same bedroom-closet mirrors, and I see a sixty-year-old body dying a little more every day. Who can I find to love that body that disgusts me more than Karen Goodpasture's puckered ass in my bedroom mirror?

My mother was not quite twenty-eight that summer. That means she was seventeen when I was born, barely seventeen—maybe even sixteen—when I was conceived. There was no doubt a shotgun wedding involved, although I've never done the math. I don't even know what month my parents were married. The anniversary wasn't an occasion to be celebrated in the Dirks household. Dear Papa ducked out before I was old enough to form a memory of him, and that same inadequate memory cannot see my mother as young as she would truly have been in 1957. Care made her seem older than she was, no doubt. She worked, I played, thinking it was all about summer fun, adventure, and vacation. I worshipped Lucy Claycomb, my own little Princess SummerFallWinterSpring. I got to watch TV every day. I got to sit in the air-conditioned lobby of the Arlington Hotel for an hour every Monday-through-Friday afternoon, and sometimes on a Saturday or Sunday my mother would buy me a Grapette and a Slo Poke and let me take them to the little park across the street from the Arlington—the same park where fifty years later I listened to a band play Sousa marches and Irving Berlin tunes and met Karen Goodpasture for the first time— as my mother put in another hour at the hotel. It was several years later, back in Little Rock, me a teenager by then, that my mother told me that she was going to have to take a second job to pay for my books and clothes for high school. "I'm sorry, Johnny," she said, fighting tears. "I hate it, having to leave you alone so much of the day. I've fought it all these years, but I'm just going to have to take a second job." "Don't worry about it, Ma," I said. "Besides, it's not like it's the first time. Don't you remember that hour you put in every afternoon at the Arlington Hotel in Hot Springs?" She was off the couch and then back down, slumped over with her arm thrown across her eyes, before I realized that she'd slapped me across the face. She was bawling so hard I could barely understand the few choked words that got out: something to the effect that she couldn't believe I actually thought she was taking money for it, that I thought she was a whore. I had been a naïve ten year old in Hot Springs, and I was still a naïve fifteen year old. But about the same time she stopped crying, I finally understood—or at least understood as much as I was capable of back then. There had been a jowly man with wavy black hair and sideburns. He reminded me of Elvis, although he was much older than Elvis, those sideburns and that surly lower lip. Had she known him before the summer in Hot Springs? Was he the reason we'd come? I didn't know. I'd seen him once or twice at the hotel, and I vaguely recalled him being at the door of our basement apartment, and my mother crying, but I thought it was because we were going to have to leave Hot Springs. I cried, too.

You still see it written in shaving cream on the car windows of the just-married:
  WEDDING TODAY, HOT SPRINGS TONIGHT!!
Yes, Hot Springs is a honeymoon destination for Arkies and Okies and Missourians who can't afford Hawaii. They stay in condos on the lake and at night heat things up—you bet!—and in the day they ride those Jet Skis. *Vroom vroom!*

I was in the third grade when a friend told me about sex—or at least a third-grade version of the sexual act. It was the most ridiculous thing I'd ever heard, and I refused to believe it. I told him he was stupid, he was crazy, he was lying, but he just grinned that infuriating grin and told me to ask my parents about it. I told him we couldn't be friends anymore if he didn't take it all back, but he just kept on grinning, so we weren't friends anymore. A half-dozen years later, when my mother slapped my face and I finally had an inkling of what had happened in the Arlington Hotel, all I could think of was what my friend had said: the man puts his wee-wee into the woman's wee-wee and shakes it around until a seed comes out. By age fifteen I was able to embellish this account with images from line drawings found in men's room stalls and photos from the "girlie magazine" one of my classmates brought to school. I pictured my mother with enormous tits and a nest of black hair between her legs, the jowly man with a dick like a donkey and his mouth on her nipples. I began to hate her a little then, and I think she knew it. She probably figured I hated her because I thought she'd taken money to sleep with the man, but my reasons were much more direct and elemental: I hated her because she disgusted me, fucking that jowly man. Fucking him, fucking him, fucking him all summer long. Disfigured by my disgust, she never fucked another man, never even had a date so far as I know. She mopped people's floors and cleaned their toilets and—knees and knuckles swollen from arthritis, gap-toothed, rheumy-eyed and hair thinning—died a lonely old woman when all she'd wanted was love. And I am so sorry. I am so sorry. The gods must truly hate us, or they never would have arranged things so that understanding always comes too late.

Hot Springs advertises itself as the destination for family fun, but at its heart is Bathhouse Row where for over a century now the maimed and twisted and infirm have come to give themselves up to the healing waters from which the city takes its name. They line up in their cars at the corner of Reserve and Central and fill up plastic milk jugs from the fountain there, the thermal waters steaming out of the spigots. The more well-heeled among Hot Springs' visitors go for the massages and mineral-water baths at the Arlington Hotel or to the Buckstaff and Quapaw Bathhouses, the only currently operating ones from among the more than half-dozen that once led Hot Springs to boast that it outshone the *Badens* of Europe. In those days the swells came down from Chicago, Cleveland, and St. Louis and spent the summer. I don't suppose anyone does anymore. Except me. These days, summer coming to a close, I haunt Bathhouse Row in search of healing, in search of love. I come in search of Karen.

Why Karen Goodpasture or, my heart tells me, no one? I'm not sure. The heart is a silent master; it doesn't explain, only compels. Do I love her? I barely *know* her. We saw each other three or four times over the period of a week, then one evening I cooked her a vegetarian lasagna dinner, and after a bottle of wine and a Viagra, we repaired to my bedroom for some friendly old-folks sex. You know the rest. Whether I wronged her isn't the point. I never called her a whore—I'm innocent of that, thank God—but I hurt her, as I have hurt too many. Ex-wives, ex-lovers, ex-friends. My mother.

For the last twenty years of her life we lived across town from one another, Little Rock a small city, a twenty-minute drive at most. I'd see her two or three times a year. On the night she died—from congestive heart failure following breast cancer—I got a call from the nursing home saying she was in a bad way. I drove over and sat with her for a few minutes and listened to her tortured breathing: the *death rattle*. Then I left for my evening seminar, on the drive turning the words death rattle over and over in my mind, and by the time I arrived on campus I had the provisional first line or two of a very promising poem. They called me out of class with the news that she was gone. I hadn't been there when my mother died, and the guilt was terrible, but now I think that even guilt can be a sort of vanity and that the worst thing wasn't that she died without me but that she died without anyone.

I don't want to die unloved, alone. So I go in search of Karen, whom I have hurt, and if I can make it right again perhaps the world will allow me to love and be loved.

But where is she?

I've been to Fisherman's Wharf where we had dinner overlooking Lake Hamilton, and I've been to St. John's Catholic Church where, she told me, she sometimes went to mass, and I've driven up and down Garden Street, but I don't know her address.

Mostly I go to the seedy old downtown, Central Avenue, and walk north up the west side of Central and gaze in the shop and restaurant windows, tempted by ice cream but not by Josephine Tussaud's Wax Museum. (I have a vision of finding myself on display next to Jack the Ripper.) For a moment I thought I saw Karen in a line of tourists outside the Ducks in the Park office, but of course I was wrong, and I laughed at the absurdity of the idea. It may be the only time I've laughed all summer.

Where Central begins to curve westward into an area of vacant lots and cheap motels, I cross to the east side and walk back south past the bathhouses. I remember them as looking older and shabbier fifty years ago. Today, they all sport fresh coats of paint and manicured lawns even if only two are functioning. The Buckstaff does a good business in baths and massages, just like in the old days, and the Fordyce Bathhouse, restored to its former glory, is now open for tours.

It is outside the Fordyce that I finally see Karen. She's with a group of women—some social organization or church group, no doubt. Why she would want to tour the Fordyce, I'm not sure. It strikes me a little like a native of Manhattan standing in line to go up in the Empire State Building. But now that I think about it, do I really know that she's from Hot Springs? She teaches junior high, and she's here *now*, but beyond that . . . . We'd talked about literature and the arts, vegetarian stir-fries and watching sunsets over water (ol' romantic me!), but we hadn't shared much personal information. Maybe, like me, she'd come to Hot Springs just for the summer. Maybe, like me, she'd come for love.

Encouraged by that possibility, I follow Karen into the Fordyce Bathhouse.

I join a group of a dozen or so (Karen's party plus a few interlopers like myself) at one end of the lobby where a uniformed young woman (National Park Service, no doubt) is describing the "Cherub Fountain."

I'm on the other side of the group opposite Karen. She spots me immediately, nods—coolly, I think—and looks away.

The tour guide descants briefly on the history and architecture of the bathhouse, and then we leave the lobby and trail through the bathing areas (separate for men and women). The cabinets with their single aperture for the head, the big white tubs festooned with faucets and handles and shower heads seem to have materialized out of some dream of Dr. Mengele's. I shudder, and at that moment Karen looks over at me and frowns. Yes, this is going well.

The gymnasium is next. The barbells, medicine balls, climbing ropes, side horses remind me of P.E. class, as close to hell as a small, awkward, timid boy need come. Just as I'm about to give up the whole venture as a bad idea, though, our tour guide cracks some lame joke, and I smile in spite of myself, and Karen smiles, too, and, taking that for a good sign, I close in and follow right behind her as the group moves up to the second floor—more baths, wooden changing booths, apparent torture chambers that must have been some sort of sweatboxes—and I can think of nothing to say although I want to fall on my knees and plead, "Forgive me, forgive me!"

We pass into the museum and browse through the display cases, mostly photographs: the roof garden where sit men in suits, ties, and bowlers and women in ankle-length dresses and wide-brimmed hats; the music room where a woman in pearls and tortoise-shell glasses plays a grand piano and her audience—those suits and ties and long dresses and wider-brimmed hats again—listen, apparently enchanted. There is no misery in any of these photographs. All look—amazingly, unaccountably—happy.

But then comes the display of electrical instruments—wires and vacuum tubes and dials and electrodes in all manner of configurations—used to treat the ailing.

"How horrible!" I murmur, almost forgetting for a moment that Karen is beside me. When she looks at me I gesture to the display—"The length people go to . . ."—but I can't finish the sentence.

"Oh, I don't know," Karen says. "I don't know if it's horrible at all. At least they hadn't given up, had they? They had the courage to try anything to make their lives better. Somehow it gives me courage . . ."

She can't finish her sentence, either. Or maybe she has finished it. They'd all come here so filled with hope—the weak and infirm, my mother in 1957, Karen, me—and if not all found healing and forgiveness, surely some did. I have to believe that.

We go on down the hall until we are out into the bright, airy music room. Only now it's just Karen and I. The tour group has taken a different way. An accident? Or has Karen lured me after her? Vain hope, perhaps, but it occurs to me that, at my age, if you can't hope for what you don't deserve, there's really not much reason to go on.

A grand piano occupies the far end of the long room, and the ceramic-tiled floor and glass-tiled ceiling are decorated in fleur-de-lis and arabesques, just as in the museum photos. Thirty years ago the room had fallen into desuetude. In fact, not so long ago the entire Fordyce Bathhouse was little more than a shell, housing ruin. Then came the restoration.

We stand staring in the direction of the piano until Karen looks over at me and says, "You're smiling."

And I say, "Am I?" because I wasn't aware of it. I gesture vaguely: "The piano . . . I was just thinking of an old tune."

And Karen smiles now, too. "So was I! What song were you thinking of?"

And even though I hadn't really been thinking of a tune, I'll name one, any one, it won't make any difference because I know that whichever it is Karen will say, "Yes! That's the one I was thinking of!"

And I'll take her in my arms, then, and give her a kiss, or if not that I'll take her hand and lead her out of the bathhouse, and we'll climb the steep steps up to the chevroned red-brick strollway that curves through the trees on the hillside above Bathhouse Row. Here and there in little grottos mineral water gurgles up out of the earth, and, even though the waters are hot, Karen will dip her hand and offer it to me. "Drink," she'll say. And I'll drink.

CPSIA information can be obtained
at www.ICGtesting.com
Printed in the USA
JSHW012045280323
39612JS00005B/38

9 781944 528904